AF225450

This book is a work of fiction. Names, places, events and characters are fictitious in every regard. Any similarity to actual events or persons, living or dead, is purely coincidental.

Gay Dicks for Straight Chicks
Copyright©2013 Jazmin Starr
ISBN 978-1-909934-04-7
Cover art and design by Dawné Dominique

Published by
Lydian Press 2013
Find us on the World Wide Web at
www.lydianpress.com

Gay Dicks for Straight Chicks

Jazmin Starr

Lydian Press

Contents

All titles were originally published as individual eBooks by loveyoudivine Alterotica.

INTRODUCTION:

It has become a truism that a lot of heterosexual men are turned on by watching lesbian lovemaking, partly by the fantasy that they are capable of 'turning' one or both partners. The same is true of gay men and their patronage of straight porn, especially gangbang straight porn in which the viewer has a feast of male flesh on which to concentrate. Now that women are more liberated in the area of erotica it was only natural that there be an upsurge in literature involving women and gay men.

Some women admit they get off on the distinctive power play between two men, while others buy into the fantasy of monogamous gay men who 'suddenly' both fall for a woman and incorporate her into the relationship. Of course, there are as many variations on that theme as there are sexual fetishes. I'm not averse to some of the mm/f material although, for the most part, it's pure fantasy. Two monogamous gay men and a woman setting up house in co-habitation? Unlikely, except in fiction.

The route I took in my *Gay Dick for the Straight Chick* is still fantasy but I like to think it has an element of realism to it. For the most part, one of the men in the gay relationship in my stories is bisexual and therefore open to sexual relations with a woman, while the 'totally' gay partner is wary of involvement either because gay men are very suspicious of bisexual men, or perhaps because of performance anxiety. But, just as there is situational homosexuality in which a straight man will bend with the prevailing gender breeze, so gay men will do the same, whether through drunkenness, force, or general horniness. A gay mate of mine keeps telling me that dicks have no morality; gender preference being a construct of the mind.

What makes gay men so attractive to straight women?

It's a story as old as time itself: hot gay guys are great in bed, have good grooming, gym-toned bods and are as handsome as fuck. All they need is a bad woman to show them the joys of the 'other' side. The conversion may not be permanent, it may last no more than a night but oh, what a night! In some cases it may just be the experience they need to explore their bi side.

Wishful thinking? Definitely. But who among us has not harbored an unrequited crush on a gay guy somewhere in our lifetime or sighed that such and such a film star was out of our sphere because we are the wrong gender? Well, in these stories, women's passions are requited – just not always in the manner they expect.

This edition collects all five of the *Gay Dick* series, plus *Christmas Carol*, the one that started the ball rolling.

It may not be an instruction manual, but it just might give you a few ideas.

Jazmin Starr
May 2013

Glory Hole Smorgasbord

My mum and dad are fuckin' hippies although they prefer the term New Age. Whatever. Doesn't matter what words you use to describe them it means major embarrassment for their kids who had no say in the matter, especially in their own names. I got lumbered with Unity. How would you like to go through school with a name like that? Jesus, what were they thinking? They might just as well have drawn a target on my back or branded a large L on my forehead for Loser. Thank Christ I wasn't the first born because she got stuck with Chastity which is ironic since she grew up to be the biggest slut in the neighborhood. It probably would have been more appropriate for me though considering how much fuckin' sex I'm getting at present. I could just as easily have said suckin' sex, 'cause I'm not getting any of that either.

I admit it's my own fault. What do I expect when I hang around with a bunch of really hot guys who live to party and to fuck…other hot guys? You got it, I'm what is called a fag hag. I don't have a problem with the description although I know it's a putdown when straight guys use the term, but straight guys are so alien to me. Sure they like to fuck but I'm into a bit more than just spreading my legs and putting up with a bit of vaginal friction for three minutes or less. Usually much less. Or sucking dick until it spews its load into my mouth. I'll even swallow but for God's sake don't shove it so far down my throat I'll upchuck that morning's Corn Flakes and Soy milk. Don't even go near my lips if you've already had your dick up my ass.

Straight guys! God's contraceptive.

I suppose I do have my folks to thank for my open mindedness. They preached peace, love and aromatherapy all through my childhood so I was ready to embrace people's differences from about the age of five. No big deal then that I got friendly with the nerds and underdogs at school. I'm a natural outcast. I hate authority, loathe team sports, don't like to submit to bullies and just naturally drift toward the bizarre, the different, the cool.

Cool is in the mind of the beholder and I guess every group from the jocks right through to the members of the chess club consider themselves 'cool' but Cree explained that 'cool' is a state of mind not who you mix with or how much money you have or what your exam marks are. He'd know because he's the epitome of cool.

I guess I fell in love with him the day he stopped a gang of older girls from picking on me in the schoolyard over, you guessed it, my name. I was in tears, screaming at the girls to shut up. He gave them such a bollocking over their bullying that they ran off in tears as well. He smiled at me, his job well done. It was that moment I fell in love with him. I followed him around the school like a lovelorn puppy even as he and his friends attempted to shoo me away. I hung around the edges of their conversation for almost a month until one day they were discussing my favorite rock group. Cree and his best mate, Dion, were arguing over the lyrics of one of their songs and neither would give ground. From a few yards away I told them they were both wrong and quoted the correct version of the lyrics they were arguing about.

The group looked over at me, probably shocked that I could speak or that I actually had an opinion.

Cree beckoned me over. "I suppose if she's right we'd better let her join the group."

There was a bit of grizzling from one or two of the boys but Cree prevailed – he usually did. When they discovered I was correct and had a love of many of the things they did I was more heartily welcomed although Dion seemed somewhat jealous of my sway over his best friend. I suspected, without knowing how or why, the two of them were also fuck buddies.

That's how I became the official fag hag to Cree and his group. It helped me get through high school. I was still an outcast but an outcast with the coolest friends. Once they got used to me in their midst they tried shocking me with explicit stories of their sexual shenanigans but when I didn't rise to the bait they backed off. They weren't to know I used the images their tales brought to mind as masturbatory fantasy material for years, especially when they involved Cree.

It was a given we'd all apply to the same college if not the same courses and, in time, we all turned up on campus. I was a year behind, a dreary year I'd spent in high school friendless and desperate for my gay buddies. Sure, I learned a lot about straight boys that year, having nothing much else to fall back on but they didn't want to discuss the latest Kylie video or fashion or anything even remotely of interest to me once the sex was over. God I pined for the day I'd be back with Cree and the gang. Meanwhile I had to satisfy myself with catching up on the few weekends their hectic schedule allowed.

Once I hit college the gang became inseparable again. We went to parties together, bars together, dancing together, movies together, although I tended to go home alone. Cree and his mates were always picking up or buddy fucking while I learned everything there was to know about my vibrator. It really didn't hack it as someone to talk to or share experiences with and the satisfaction was only fleeting.

One night in a dark, crowded club, watching Cree and Dion snogging and more in a corner, I lost it. I screamed, "Why can't I get fucking laid?" I thought all eyes turned to me but, in reality, the music was so loud that only the people in the immediate vicinity heard me. I stormed off to the bar to get plastered. It didn't help.

Later, on the street after the club closed and while Dion was getting his car, Cree wrapped his arm around me. "Is it really that bad, Une? You not getting any?"

I pouted. "Less than zero."

"Aw, that's awful."

He held me close while I sobbed my frustration away.

"Hey, you up for an adventure?" he asked.

"Does it involve me getting laid?"

"Big time," he laughed.

"Hell, yeah."

That's how a nice girl like me found herself at an adult book shop the next night with a horny gay boy.

I was nervous as fuck. I'd never been in a place like this before. Sure I'd seen pornos, my dad had his favorites on DVD tucked away at the bottom of his underpants drawer and I'd found mum's vibrator and a couple of toys that I had no idea what to do with in her bedside table. I lost my virginity at the prom. What a cliché I am but it wasn't so much that I lost it as it was something I was pleased to get rid of. I threw it away. I knew enough that the first time you did 'it' with a boy it hurt like blazes and I had no intention of saving it for my wedding night although weddings were the last thing on my mind especially as my sister had already gone through her first and was on to her second by the time I reached fucking age.

The boy I chose to rid me of my unwanted hymen had as little idea of the mechanics as me but we fumbled through it both getting what we wanted and both ridding ourselves of the stain of virginity in the process. They say you never forget your first. Not true. I'd forgotten him before he even came.

The sex shop was a whole new experience and I guess it was how I should have felt that first time. Excitement mixed with trepidation – the sweet with the sour like a good salad dressing. I never would have done it on my own no matter how horny I was. If Cree hadn't been there I wouldn't have entered the premises let alone made my way to the porno booths at the back of the shop secreted behind a door with dangling strips of colored plastic.

My heart was thumping in my chest, I felt so naughty. Not dirty, my parents were too adult to ever describe sex as dirty. They believed it was an appetite every bit as important as eating, sleeping, or breathing.

"Take your panties off," Cree whispered.

When I hesitated he gestured with his hand that he was serious. "Come on, don't go all prudish now."

"Turn your back." I was already red in the face from embarrassment.

"For God's sake Une, you're going to see me down on my knees sucking dick in a minute you think a flash of pussy is going to worry me?"

"I thought gay men were revolted by girl's bits?"

"Nah, they just don't get us hard, that's all."

I whipped my panties off and he stuffed them in his back pocket for safe keeping. He wiped the vinyl bench so I'd have somewhere to sit before he put a dollar in the machine and some old porn movie came up on the small monitor embedded in the wall. The actors all looked bored, merely going through the motions for the pay check by the looks of it. It was about as exciting as bringing myself off with a vibrator on quarter power.

Much more interesting was watching Cree on his knees staring through the hole in the wall at whoever was in the cubicle next to ours. It was occupied because he'd tried the door to make sure it was locked before we came into this one and bolted ourselves in.

Suddenly this big hard cock began to poke through what Cree told me was called a Glory Hole. I pinched myself so I wouldn't get an attack of the giggles. I'd only ever seen a few live cocks in my life and none of them up till now had been poking through the wall like this one. Cree gave it a few tugs with his hand, wet his lips and leaned forward to take it in his mouth.

Holy shit! I was watching my very best gay friend sucking a stranger's cock through a hole drilled in a porno booth at the back of an adult book store. My first thought was not how hot it looked but rather that my parents would be so proud of me. I shook that thought from my brain, after all who wants to be thinking about their mum and dad at a moment like this?

It didn't take long at all for me to realize Cree had been right about removing my panties because watching him at work slurping over this cock lollipop was doing things to my pussy that required my fingers. No wonder he was popular, he could take the guy's cock right down to his balls without choking. I'd give anything to be able to do that.

Cree worked the cock like it was a gourmet meal, licking, sucking, swallowing, covering every inch with his lips and his tongue and his spit. The guy on the other side of the wall must have been getting close because I could hear him moaning over the partition and he was thrusting faster and faster into Cree's mouth. The guy's body was knocking frantically against the wall until he panted real loud and I saw Cree's throat muscles contracting. Holy fuck, he swallowed all his cum.

The guy pulled out and we heard him zip up and the booth door open.

Cree smiled, licking his lips. "Tasty. Nice big load."

I screwed up my face. "Gross."

He shrugged. "You don't have to swallow. I just happen to love the taste of cum."

There wasn't time to discuss the finer points of swallowing versus spitting because someone new entered the booth next door and his eye appeared at the hole. He must have liked what he saw of Cree because very soon we heard coins drop in the slot followed by the erotic sound of a zip being lowered. This guy had a foreskin, something I'd never seen in the flesh before, but which seemed to please Cree because he mouthed the word 'Yum' before pushing his tongue under the flap.

My breathing was labored as I watched and my pussy was definitely tingling from all the sounds and visuals that were going on around me. I pushed my fingers into my pussy, rubbing my thumb around my clit, making myself even wetter than I was already. I must have moaned because Cree looked up from his task and smiled at me raising an eyebrow that I was still covering myself modestly with my skirt. Well why not? He still had all his clothes on.

He was enjoying this cock a lot more than the first one as I could hear him sort of humming as his head bobbed up and down the shaft. He looked so good I wished I had a movie of it so I could copy his technique. I was surprised when the guy withdrew his cock because he obviously hadn't blown his load, then I saw his index finger come through the hole beckoning Cree. I wondered what that was all about until Cree unbuckled his jeans and peeled them down.

I didn't know where to look and closed my eyes until I remembered that was why I was here in the first place.

Sure, I'd seen Cree's cock before but never like this. He lifted the front of his T-shirt up and over his head so it showed off his hot muscular body as well as giving me an uninterrupted view of his magnificent cock and balls. He pushed his cock through the hole and I felt like busting into the booth next door and sucking the cum out of his balls myself. Instead I watched his hard tanned butt move back and forth as the lucky fucker on the other side got to suck the man I adored. I just hoped Cree didn't come too quickly. I was just getting into the swing of it.

Just as I thought it was all going to be over, Cree withdrew and kneeled, waiting for his partner to poke his cock through again. Cree's eyes looked all dreamy and sexed and he attacked the cock with new energy as if he was trying to suck every ounce of spunk from the guy's balls. He looked over to see what I was up to and seemed pleased that I was frigging my pussy, my skirt up around my belly now, my pussy as unencumbered as his cock.

As he continued to suck the anonymous cock, he surprised me by running his hand along my thigh until he reached my pussy lips. Instead of retreating as I expected he would he ran his finger up and down the slit and then plunged into my wetness. I couldn't believe what was happening. It was like I was on drugs.

Fortunately, the booth was so tiny I was in easy reach of him and he continued to plunge two fingers into my sopping cunt while he continued to drain the guy through the glory hole. I wanted to make the moment last but I knew a shuddering orgasm was just around the corner. Suddenly Cree took his lips off the cock, dragged me from the vinyl seat where I was perched and whispered for me to finish the guy off. I was so hot for cock I didn't hesitate. Sure, I wasn't as expert but I didn't think the guy on the other side of the wall was going to complain as long as I kept my teeth out of it.

Cree manhandled me into position on my knees until I could comfortably reach the cock which I began to lick in an imitation of his technique before I wrapped my mouth around it and sucked. Cree found my cunt again and buried his fingers inside me fucking me gently as I flexed my muscles wishing it were his cock I was gripping. Fuck I was an ungrateful bitch. I never expected to get this far with him and just to have his fingers…shit, I'd been concentrating so much on my own pleasure I'd forgotten my partner until I heard him cuss and felt a flood of warm slime coat my tongue.

I wanted Cree to be proud of me so I swallowed. It wasn't so bad, although it wasn't so good either. I barely had time to notice because Cree brought me to the edge and toppled me over. For a gay guy he sure had magic fingers and I was surprised he played my pussy so well. I shuddered as my cunt flooded with more satisfaction than I'd felt in months and the cock gave one last small twitch and then disappeared back through the hole.

I slumped back against my heels wondering if either of us was going to give way to embarrassment. I needn't have worried because Cree was still horny. When we heard a new occupant enter the booth he lifted me off the floor back onto the bench and put his eye to the hole. He must have liked what he saw because he stood and inserted his cock in the hole in the wall, thrusting back and forth into what must have been a man's mouth on the other side.

All this sexual excitement was doing my head in and I was constantly aroused although I wanted more than anything to have contact with Cree even though I knew he was totally gay. My cunt was dripping as I watched his beautiful prick disappear into the hole and his ass bob back and forth. I'd heard enough stories about Cree's sex life that I knew he liked cock in his ass. Or toys or even fingers to help get him off.

Did I dare?

I dipped my fingers into my sopping pussy then using the juices as lubrication I parted Cree's ass cheeks quickly and pushed my fingers against his tight butt hole. My two fingers slid in fairly easily and he gasped in surprise but made no attempt to free himself.

"Put another finger in," he panted as he thrust his ass back against my hand.

Using more of my cunt juice to slick my fingers I pushed against his sphincter. His ass was tighter this time but eventually they were in to the second knuckle and then all the way. I fucked in and out as he pushed his dick into the glory hole, him gasping with pleasure now that he had it at both ends. I couldn't believe that I was getting it on with the gay boy I'd fancied for so long. Without even touching myself I felt an orgasm building, I shuddered fit to bring the house down as it wracked my body. It took a lot of concentration to keep my fingers embedded in his tight butthole until he dumped his spunk in the guy's throat. I heard him whimper then his ass muscles gripped my fingers so I knew he was unloading. The spasms seemed to last an age.

Cree pulled his softening cock back through the hole and I reluctantly extracted my fingers from his ass.

"Fuck, Une, that was so intense. Where did you learn to do that?"

I smiled. "From listening to you guys."

"Wait until I tell the others," he said.

"You wouldn't?"

"Hell, yeah. Why not?"

"Won't you be embarrassed that you did it with a girl?"

"Are you embarrassed, is that it?"

"No," I lied. I really didn't know what I was.

"If you are…"

"No, I'm not embarrassed. At least I don't think I am. It's all so new to me."

He pulled up his trousers. "Let's get out of here and grab a coffee."

"Okay."

We ended up talking for hours about what had just happened. Cree seemed to think it was little more than a natural progression in our friendship. Of course, I saw it as much more. He must have realized because he took my hand and said gently, "I know you have feelings for me, Une, but it's not going to happen. I like you a lot but I'm gay. Sure I can do things with a girl but it's who I fall in love with that makes me gay, not where I put my cock. My heart and my cock have separate lives. You understand?"

"I think so."

He saw my disappointment. "Hey, cheer up. There are other guys in the group who would love to fuck you."

"Really?"

"You mean you haven't noticed? Kevin is sooo hot for you."

"He's cute."

"And it doesn't mean we can't play round from time to time. Dion isn't always around when I need him."

In fact, Dion disappeared a lot after Cree revealed our little up-close-and-familiar. Seems he didn't mind sharing with other guys but a chick finger fucking his part-time boyfriend brought on a major attack of the sulks. That meant more Cree for me.

Sure, I tried it on with Kevin who was hot in bed and liked to share me with his current boyfriend. They liked to do me together but I was strictly invited on an ad hoc basis which suited me fine as I still pined for Cree. With Dion as moody as fuck Cree and I managed to repeat our experience at the sex shop.

We carried on like two school kids rather than the young adults we were. I slipped out of my panties as soon as we barricaded ourselves in the booth waiting for a stranger on either side. We moved up a notch and ensconced ourselves in a booth with a glory hole on either side – one each, according to Cree.

Yeah, I admit we'd been drinking and flirting heavily with each other. Cree slipped a coin into the machine and a porno whirred to life. Neither of us was interested much, my eyes were fixed on Cree who was removing all his clothes making it the first time I had seen him totally naked. Shit, my pussy ached for him. The man is so fucking gorgeous.

"Come on," he encouraged. "Your turn."

I was pissed enough to join him. He pinched my nipples which were pebble hard already and then, to my surprise he leaned over and sucked each in turn until my pussy flooded with my first orgasm of the night. He was hard and I wrapped my hand round his shaft and tugged but he took my hand off, whispering that he didn't want to come yet.

There was a whole different atmosphere this time: more playful but also more serious. Yeah, that's a contradiction but it's the only way I can explain it. I knew we'd go further this time but I also knew it was for fun not for 'real.'

"I need to get fucked real bad, Une," he said.

"Me, too," I agreed.

He took a small tube of lubrication from the pocket of his jeans which he'd folded on the bench. "Here, lube me up."

He squeezed a generous glob on my fingers before he turned around and bent over parting his ass cheeks with his hands. I ran my slimy fingers down his crack to his puckered hole and pushed. He sighed, my fingers worming their way inside him until he was thrusting back against my hand. "That feels so good," he moaned.

He stood up and turned his attention to me. His fingers found my clit and his thumb traced a circle making me flinch before he drove two fingers into me. I was already wet and his manipulation threatened to flood my cunt with more of my juices.

"Hey, no fair. You're already way ahead of me."

At that moment a cock pushed through the glory hole on his side. Cree kneeled to spit lube it quickly before he stood to back up against the thick veiny cock. He sucked in his breath as it breached his hole and exhaled contentedly as he speared himself to the wall. I was envious as he rocked back and forth against the prick that was embedded totally inside him. I crawled beneath him and watched the cock enter him stretching his ass lips until they looked as if they would snap. It was times like this I wish I had a cock.

"Don't look now but I think you have an admirer," he gasped.

There was a cock begging attention from the glory hole on my side of the booth. I was so horny there was only one way to satisfy me and without any further ado I backed onto the monster, sinking it right into my wet cunt.

The guy on the other side of the wall let out a "Holy fuck," as I tightened my pussy muscles around his throbbing weapon. He slammed into me as Cree and I bent forward, our heads touching in the confines of the small booth. I opened my mouth and his tongue sought it out, thrusting between my lips. I sucked it gently wishing it were his cock.

People may think what we were doing was gross but to me it had become the most natural and wonderful thing in the world. I was sharing with a gay boy I loved. I was getting right royally fucked and I'd got my fingers in his ass again. Might not sound like much but oh my God…

There was a lot of heavy breathing and then scuffles from the other side of Cree then I saw him stand to stretch his muscles. He had obviously scored a load in his butt because he pushed his finger inside then sucked it clean.

"You up for a competition?" he whispered, a wicked gleam in his eye.

"What sort of competition?"

"See who can take the most loads in, say, the next hour?"

"You're on. What's the bet?"

"Loser has to suck the loads out of the winner."

The thought of winning and having Cree's lips on my cunt made me lose it. I came bucket loads squeezing the cock inside me until it blew its load. The poor guy just kept mumbling "Jesus. Jesus," over and over until I felt him withdraw.

Cree kneeled down to his glory hole and whispered to the guy who'd just fucked him. "Hey, mate. Tell anyone in the shop who's interested, there's two sluts in this booth looking to take as much cock as they can get in the next hour. Me on this side, a cunt on the other. Okay?"

"You sure you know what you're getting yourself into," his trick asked.

"Can't get enough cock tonight."

"It's your ass and her cunt," he said just before he left the cubicle.

Cree brought out the best and the worst in me so for the next hour or so we took on any cock that poked through our respective glory holes, no questions asked. It was dirty, it was exciting, and it was fucking awesome. We both sweated like pigs as we took more and more cock, Cree complaining, "You've got an advantage, you've got two holes."

I laughed. "I'm only using one, does that make it fairer?"

Naturally, the count had to be honor system because there was no way of counting each other's loads. We giggled as cocks breached the glory holes impaling his ass and my cunt on their stiffness, sometimes getting so turned on by the constant shagging that his eyes glazed over or my body convulsed with another orgasm. His cock was hard the whole time he was being fucked, drooling pre-cum that I wished I could taste.

I knew I was losing the count and I didn't fancy sucking all those guys' loads out of his ass, it turned my stomach but I didn't know what I could do. My head was in a strange place. Here I was, a young woman, her pussy up against a particle board wall in a sex shop getting gang fucked in a competition with a gay guy. Could life get any better?

Yeah, it could. There were still guys in the corridor chatting excitedly as the hour was up. Cree took one last load and a few minutes later my guy finished off. His cum dripped between my legs even though I tried to hold it in.

"Okay, how many?" he asked.

"I think it was twelve. I might have lost count in the middle."

He sounded surprised. "So, it could be more?"

"Maybe one or two." Was I boasting or was I admitting to being a slut?

"Damn!" he said, although he didn't sound too upset.

"What do you mean, 'Damn'?"

"I only managed eleven," he said, a look of mock sorrow on his face. "How can I face my mates?"

"I win?"

"Looks like it. Okay, sit on the bench."

I sat on the vinyl bench heavily. Surely he wasn't going to go through with it?

Kneeling between my legs, he placed them over his shoulders. He smiled at me like a naughty boy, took a deep breath and plunged his mouth down onto my leaking twat. It was like an electric charge shot through my body as his tongue sought my slit and pushed inside. He found my clit, licking and sucking gently until I was bucking on the bench. He surprised me when he put his mouth against my cunt entrance and began to suction the cum into his mouth. Every now and then he would take his lips off my sore pussy and lick between my legs getting every drop of sperm he could, his mouth and chin glistening with the combination of my juices and that of the guys who fucked me.

I must have been drained of all their loads but Cree kept right on. I realized he was trying to make me come with his tongue. I relaxed into it and let the fantasy and the reality meld watching the beautiful gay boy working my cunt like an expert. I squeezed my legs around his head holding him in place as I felt the shudder begin, my orgasm flooding his mouth making his face sticky with my juice.

I panted, almost unable to move. Cree grinned like a kid who stole a pie. He stood up, his cock as erect as it had been all night. He didn't ask. I didn't want him to. He slid his greasy prick into my mouth, holding my head still as he thrust a little farther into my throat each time until I could no longer breathe. I didn't panic and he pulled out quickly so that I didn't gag. I made no complaint because I never dreamed I would have his cock inside me, even if it was just my mouth. I took him as best I could which must have been good enough because he groaned as he thrust faster, nearing his peak, and then I felt the splash of his warm salty cum on my tongue and I sucked until the final squirts hit the back of my throat.

Then like the good girl I am, I swallowed.

I swallowed more and more over the next few years although never again Cree's load. There were other gay boys who were less gay and more straight who were more than happy to fuck a sympathetic pussy. If it sounds like I got the dregs or I was a pity fuck, nothing could be farther from the truth. We were young, we were experimenting and we mixed genders as often as we mixed numbers of participants.

Cree always remained elusive. We never went back to the sex shop again. Well, not together. Occasionally I'd drop in hoping to catch him at one of his favorite haunts but he was never there when I was although I knew he still patronized the place. The assistant at the front counter told me so. Cree was notorious for his behavior and was always welcome when he was in one of his horny moods, once sucking off every male in the store before it closed.

I tried a few times on my own but it just wasn't the same.

The culmination of my time with the gang was the year Cree graduated. It was his birthday and he and Dion had decided to head overseas together for a year or two before deciding where their futures lay. The other guys were now about to get jobs as accountants, doctors and even a lawyer in the big wide world after a little more hands-on training.

I still had that year that I was always behind. Cree promised me I was welcome to join him and Dion wherever they were in the world after I'd graduated in my chosen field, teaching disabled children.

The raucous party for Cree's twenty-second birthday was a lavish affair. Dion's family had donated their mansion overlooking the harbor for the evening, conveniently going away for the weekend so we wouldn't be disturbed. Dion himself invited me although I got the distinct impression he'd prefer it if I didn't come. Fuck him; I wouldn't miss this for the world.

It was a warm night, the breeze blowing off the harbor keeping the temperature in the comfort range. The party was mainly made up of hot guys with a small smattering of girls. One, Sabrina, caught my eye. She was dressed entirely in black leather and wore boots with the sort of high heels that threatened to topple a lesser woman. She gravitated to me as if she recognized a kindred soul.

"You must be Unity," she said. "I've heard lots of interesting stories about you." She smiled as she said it, no trace of sarcasm in her voice.

"What sort of birthday party is this?" I asked.

"Not the usual kind. Cree's asked all his friends to fuck him as a farewell – a sort of going away present."

"Damn," I said. "That leaves me out. I don't have a dick."

As the night progressed and the crowd got louder and drunker, men huddled around Cree on a divan at one end of the room. Earlier, he spent time with me and we had a little cry that we were going to be split up for a year or so but we knew our friendship would survive the separation. The university year was over, we were all going to scatter to various parts of the globe except for me: I was staying put for another twelve months. I would miss my friends, the guys I'd grown up with, who had helped form my personality, who had fucked me even though they were gay or perhaps a little bit straight-ish, who had even taught me how to handle straight men.

I'd settled into a number of longish relationships with guys some of whom were content with one partner of the opposite sex but some who changed sides as often as they changed their underwear. I kept remembering Cree's words about it not being your genitals that dictated your preference but rather your heart. I wasn't a jealous woman and I'd long since given up any hope of attracting Cree. He was a close friend with whom I'd shared and I would share one last time at the party, although I didn't know that until Sabrina came to me while I watched lovingly as Dion and Kevin fucked Cree on the carpet in the center of the room.

"He's insatiable tonight," Sabrina said. "I think he's taken something to help him. He'll be horny all night. There's not enough cock in the neighborhood to satisfy him."

I laughed. "He envied me once when we had a competition to see who could drain the most cocks in an hour because I had two holes to his one. More than anything he wanted a male vagina just for the night. Tonight I wish I had a cock."

I thought I'd said something wrong as Sabrina dragged me to one of the upstairs bedrooms. "Your wish can come true tonight, my dear," she said.

By the time I walked back downstairs again the party was noisier than ever. Cree was begging for someone to fuck him, lying on his back, his ass hoisted in the air to attract any stray cock, pearls of cum drooling from his pink hole.

"I'll fuck you," I shouted over the noise.

All eyes turned in my direction and a few of the guys let out a whoop when they saw me. I was naked except for the black leather knee-high boots Sabrina had loaned me, and the large black dildo that stuck out from around my groin, the other end of it buried in my cunt.

Cree watched as I advanced on him like a predatory animal. I was going to get my wish at long last, although not quite in the manner I expected. I saw Dion's look of indecision but it was too late to stop me now. I could read in Cree's eyes that he wanted it as much as I did. He pulled his legs higher to give me access to his plundered asshole. I kneeled, positioning the dildo head at his entrance. He was slick with his mates' spunk. I'd lubricated the dildo upstairs so that it slid easily between his sphincter muscles.

He grunted as the rubber cock was larger than I'd seen on any of the men tonight and I knew it must hurt a little.

"Oh, fuck, that's good," he whispered. "Give it to me, baby. Fuck me hard."

I moved my pelvis, the dildo penetrating him until I was pressed against his skin, the other end of the strap-on buried deep inside me. I picked up the pace slamming 'my' cock into him like I'd always wanted him to do to me, leaning down to kiss him as he took me without complaint. I was opening him up for anyone else who wanted him tonight but for the next few minutes he was mine.

He was focused on me and the way I was making him feel, the way I was playing his ass. "Make me come. Please," he begged.

Running my hands across his body, I pinched his nipples hard until he thrashed against the pain, all the while keeping up the assault on his butt. The cunt end of the dildo was driving me wild and I hoped the end shoved up his ass felt as good against his prostate. It was awesome dominating my favorite gay boy, fucking him into submission, listening to the mewling from his throat as the friction brought him closer to orgasm. I knew I could do it. I could make him spill his spunk all over his chest, something all the guys born with cocks between their legs had failed to do.

I increased the speed and thrust until I had him grunting every time my body slapped against his, my own need to come building inside me as I knew his was in him. I looked him in the eye and even though his were glazed with lust I knew he was conscious of getting the fucking of his life. He would never forget this night, he would never forget me. If I couldn't possess him then no man would ever possess him totally either because this fuck and what we'd shared in the sex shop would always be part of us, something only we could share.

He howled like a coyote as cum spurted from his cock, coating his chest and stomach. I was less vocal but no less explosive as my pussy flooded with my excitement. I saw stars. The world spun out of control as I rammed him into the carpet hoping it would never end.

But end it did as we both lay exhausted, the partygoers whispering among themselves as I pulled out of Cree's gaping ass. Dion kneeled to wipe the cum off his boyfriend's body, actually smiling at me in what I thought was admiration. I stood on unsteady feet to make my way upstairs to return the device that had given us both so much pleasure.

"Keep it," Sabrina said. "You're way better at it than I ever was. You're a natural."

Now I have to decide whether to pack it or not. What if Customs open my bags? Fuck it. In it went with my swimwear. I'm sure I can talk my way out of it if it's illegal.

One year on and I was heading to Santorini for my summer holidays to join Cree and Dion before I settled down to my teaching career. I'd already applied for numerous positions and had been accepted by a rather prestigious institution. I was looking forward to the beginning of the school year in February.

Until then…

"Please come and join us," Cree wrote. "Santorini is chock full of the hottest gay boys you'll ever meet. And Dion and I have 'met' quite a few already. The atmosphere here is very casual and some of the gay boys are not quite as gay as they make out. So, there's plenty of opportunity for you to make out with them, especially if you bring that delightful apparatus of yours. And maybe if Dion goes sailing one day and we stay back in the hotel, who knows…?"

Welcome To Paradise

Almost since the day we were married, my husband, Leith, had been badgering me – to sleep with another man. Why would I want to? Leith is the closest thing to God you're ever going to find on this earth. Muscles coming out his ears, but not the sort of overblown walnuts that professional bodybuilders like to show off, just those firm biceps with that lovely vein running across them. The sort of look that makes you feel protected when he puts his arms around you.

His chest is a whole encyclopedia of muscle and he does, indeed, have washboard abs that I love to rub my pussy over when I'm feeling particularly adventurous. His ass is so perfect he was once asked by an artist if he could paint it. Poor Leith went the color of a London post box and politely declined, although he did offer mine up as long as he could watch, obviously hoping there was more than just paint and canvas involved.

Of course, you're dying to know about the angle of the dangle between his powerful thighs. It's a very satisfying eight inches. I know because once, in a moment of madness, I took a tape measure to bed to compare figures with my girlfriends' about their partners' length and girth. Leith won hands down in both departments. He's not as round as a beer can but it's certainly a handful as well as a mouthful.

So why would he want to watch me with another man? Two possibilities. He's gay? Scratch that one, he's as red blooded a heterosexual as they come, and he comes quite often. Perhaps bi. Definitely not gay. So the reason he wants to see me paired off with another man is because his cock is itchy to try out some other fanny?

Over my dead body. No way will I give him permission to play around. He might find someone better than me.

"I don't want to play around with other women, I love you, honey." He always pleaded like a little boy. It didn't make me any more inclined to believe him.

I talked it over with my best girlfriend, Sue. She was so envious I thought she'd explode. "Shit, I'd give five years off my life to have a hubby who encouraged me to fuck around. I'd give ten years to have a hubby like Leith. Mmmm. You don't know how lucky you are, Hazel," she said.

Lucky? I don't think so.

"He just wants to dip that big schlong of his in some other woman's pussy."

"Is that what he said?"

"No, he wants to watch and maybe join in."

"What? Fuck the other guy while he's screwing you to the bed?" Sue's breath was getting decidedly labored throughout the conversation and if she hadn't both hands atop the café table I would have sworn she was diddling herself.

"This conversation is turning you on." I was horrified by the thought. "By the idea of my husband with another man."

"Anyone's husband with another man, not just yours."

I winced. "Ewww."

"In fact any men in any number and any position together."

"Since when did you become a pervert?"

"There speaks a woman who has obviously never looked at gay men porn."

"I refuse to answer on the grounds that it may make me sound like a prude."

"Oh, honey, you don't know what you're missing."

"I have a man, thanks, I don't need anything more."

"Doesn't Leith get turned on by the idea of two women together?"

I mumbled my response.

"What?"

I sighed in exasperation. "Yes, he does."

"So why shouldn't women get turned on by watching two men?"

"Because with Leith and all other men, they probably think that what they have tucked away in their undies is all that it would take to turn those lesbians straight."

"Just like women who watch gay porn believe subconsciously that all a gay man needs to turn him straight is what's down her knickers."

"I've never had any desire to get a gay man to switch teams."

That was Friday. By the end of the following week I had done a total about face.

Sue came over for a porn afternoon on Sunday while Leith and his mates played their weekly footie match against some other suburban husbands eager to escape home life, so we had a few spare hours alone. She arrived well-armed with gay and bisexual porn. It all began embarrassingly, me not knowing where to look until it was impossible not to admire the chiseled bodies and the alarmingly huge cocks on the actors who put Leith to shame.

"Wouldn't that make your eyes water?" Sue said as one guy with more muscles than stubble rammed his gigantic dick up some young blond twink. That was a new word I'd learned already; a twink being a male bimbo.

"Oh, come on," I grimaced. "His cock must concertina, there's no way he'll get that monster into the young guy's…holy fuck!"

There was a lot more of that type of comment as the afternoon progressed. Yep, it seems gay men could get huge cocks into the smallest asses and the smallest mouths with enough lubrication and enough perseverance. I had to admire the stamina and the high pain threshold of the guys on the receiving end.

"I only ever let Leith screw me in the ass once. It hurt so much I thought I was shitting gravel for the next week. Never again."

"You are missing a truly extraordinary experience by cutting off that area of sexual experience," Sue said.

"You and Alan…?"

"Good Lord, no. Alan can barely drag himself away from the television to do his husbandly duty for birthdays and Christmas let alone give me a good butt fuck."

I was learning a lot about my best friend that, I think, I would have preferred left in the privacy of a sleazy motel room.

Sue changed movies and soon we were in the throes of a bisexual free-for-all and this time my breathing did become a little labored and my pussy moist. I actually began to wish Sue would suddenly remember an urgent appointment and leave, forgetting to take her DVD rentals with her. No such luck. The sound of two women heavy breathing is not something easily disguised and I broke out in a panic that Sue might become so turned on she'd make a lunge at me.

All right, I was prepared to admit that two or more men fucking themselves hoarse were a definite cunt tingle, but the idea of pussy wrangling with my best friend was a step way, way too far. I was trying to think of some way to break the mood when the movie did it for me.

I shrieked. "She can't possibly take three cocks at once. Where's she gonna put…oh my God! The goddamn dirty bitch. How does she do that?"

Sue laughed at my discomfort as my body writhed painfully at the thought of taking a dick in my ass, my cunt and my mouth simultaneously. I have nothing against oral sex, I'm quite proud of my prowess and Leith has never complained although I have to admit my technique is much less enthusiastic than what some of these movie actors got up to. Only once did Leith ever get his cock down my throat and to this day he swears it was an accident but it felt too much like suffocating for me to repeat it. Now I hold on to his dick with my hand at the base so he can't push it all the way in.

Sue was sarcastic. "That must be so satisfying for him."

"You deep throat?" I guess I shouldn't have sounded so amazed because Sue took umbrage.

"Of course I do. Let me rephrase that, I did. I was pretty good at it to. And, before you ask, I swallowed."

I screwed my face up in disgust. Who was this alien creature seated beside me? How well did I really know my best friend?

"It's all very well for you to screw your face up like that but I never had the luxury of your looks and your tits. If you're not beautiful like you are then attracting eligible men is a lot harder. One way of doing it is if you get a reputation for doing things that nice girls won't."

"Like swallow their junk?"

"Uh huh."

That was another thing Leith was always begging me to do, swallow his cum. "I hate it in my mouth and spit it out as fast as possible."

Sue looked shocked. "That is so rude."

I could sense an argument brewing. I needed to change the subject. Nodding my head toward the screen, I asked, "You ever done anything like that?"

Sue visibly relaxed. "Three men at once? Tick. Deep throat a dick? Tick. One in my mouth with one in my pussy? Tick. One in my mouth with another one in my ass? Tick. Double penetration? Tick, tick."

I suddenly felt my sexual education was sorely lacking. Maybe that was the reason Leith wanted me to fuck another man, so I might learn a few new techniques.

I was so horny by the time Sue left with her little collection of sexual stimulation, refusing to leave a sample so I could watch in private and bring my frustration to a shattering end. "I have to get these movies back to my gay friend, Michael. He doesn't like them out of his sight for too long."

No matter. I was pretty sure my memory of them would do the trick and I could edit and fast forward in my mind. Fortunately, Leith came home before I had a chance so I attacked him, putting a little of my new knowledge to good use.

"What got into you?" he gasped when I'd had my third orgasm of the evening. "I was beginning to think you were a clone and that my real wife had been taken away by aliens."

"Am I boring sex, honey?" I asked.

The flicker of absolute terror across his face told me I'd hit a nerve. What could he do? He lied. "Of course not, honey. It's just that anything we humans keep repeating is bound to lose a bit of its excitement. After all, you wouldn't think much of pizza if it's all you ever had for dinner."

"Are you comparing our lovemaking to pizza?" I swear he had all the subtlety of a tap dancing pachyderm.

He backtracked and groveled until I had to forgive him because the way he slipped his cock between my cunt lips distracted me, as he fully intended. When it came to a choice between cock and pizza, my husband's prick won every time. Write me in twenty years and see if I still feel the same.

In this disposable age, ten years was remarkable longevity in a relationship, especially with a husband as heavily fancied as mine is. He was constantly hit upon by women of all ages and quite a few men but, as far as I could ascertain, he had never strayed. Remarkable when you consider opportunity not only knocked, it battered down the bloody door.

Yes, his constant mentions of introducing a little spice to our relationship irritated but as Sue pointed out, 'At least he's not asking to introduce another woman.' There was that.

"If another man came sniffing around me, you'd rip his head off," I chided Leith on the umpteenth occasion he brought up the subject.

"Not true," he said. "Depends on the way he goes about it. If you started having a clandestine affair with, say, a guy at work, yeah, I'd beat the shit out of him. Honey, I'm not talking about cheating, I'm talking about two adults openly extending their sexual horizons. A relationship that's built on trust. Honesty."

"Doesn't matter what terms you couch it in, the answer is still 'no.' I couldn't stand watching you with another woman."

"I don't want another woman," he emphasized yet again. "It's about watching you being pleasured…"

"By a man who's not my husband!"

We always got into an argument whenever he brought up the subject which he seemed to do with more regularity than previously. It was almost an obsession.

"Look," he said, attempting to defuse the situation. "I trust you, I have enough self confidence that you love me and any little extra-curricular activity on the side would not change our feelings for each other. I have enough faith in your love."

It was the same discussion every time, just expressed in slightly different words. Leith probably hoped to wear down my resistance through repetition. It would never have worked except for that afternoon of man-on-man action movies curated by my perfidious friend, Sue, who I began to suspect was in Leith's pay. Why else would she fuck with my mind like she had?

But I did go out and buy a number of DVDs from an adult bookshop, even plucking up the courage to ask the obviously gay gent behind the counter which gay DVDs women were most likely to buy. Con was a true professional and we spent an amazing thirty minutes discussing our preferences of the male porn actors who adorned the covers of various movies. It seems we had similar tastes and I wondered about popping the question if he'd like to come home and ram his cock up my dripping fanny in front of my gob smacked husband. But I didn't. I was tempted because he was a good match for Leith in the looks and the body department. From what I could see of his prominent bulge he had Leith's equivalent snoozing behind the fly to his jeans as well.

"When you've finished with this lot," Con said as he handed over my goods wrapped in a plain brown paper bag, "Bring them back and you can swap them for new ones at half price. A lot of women do that."

I thanked him profusely, taking my guilty purchases and putting my head down as I exited to the street hoping no one I knew saw me. After a secretive afternoon with me, my vibrator and my new movie collection, plus a number of intense orgasms that should have rattled the windows, I still had enough energy left to tackle Leith as soon as he came home. After another powerful session of lovemaking during which I wondered what it would be like to have a cock even larger than my husband's rammed into my dripping pussy, he said, "I don't know what's got into you lately, but whatever it is, keep it up."

Of course, the lure of the sex emporium and Con's supportive and very conducive company were too much for me to ignore and I made many a furtive safari to swap movies and gossip, slowly opening up about my personal life to Con who became a surrogate father confessor figure. He'd seen it all in his years in the shop, and now at the ripe old age of thirty he had a delightfully smutty acceptance of people's foibles. I was to discover that Leith's was all-too-common.

"Honey, most women would be so envious of you. Husbands usually want another woman."

"So my good friend, Sue, told me."

"Your man is just so proud of you he wants to show you off. He wants other men to be envious of the gorgeous woman he loves and who loves him back unconditionally."

It always seemed so simple the way Con explained it but once I left the shop it got all complicated again. As the weeks went by I found myself changing. When it came to the bedroom I was more vulgar and demanding, a change that Leith welcomed wholeheartedly, although not without a certain wariness as to what had brought about the change. He tried wheedling it out of me but I bamboozled him with a female pseudo-medical condition that supposedly increased a woman's libido. Any time he became too suspicious, I simply swallowed an extra inch or two of his cock and swallowed his spunk which I found to be far less gross than I had remembered. I'd have to think of another method shortly because I was now comfortably taking his prick almost to the base without gagging.

What sat much less comfortably with me were the fantasies that flashed through my mind. Men I'd seen in the street or the office or the shops who I found particularly attractive during the day were elbowing their way into my lovemaking at night when I imagined them fucking me instead of Leith. Of more concern was the number of times the fantasy lover became Con.

I cursed the day Leith had ever brought up the subject because it preoccupied so much of my waking thought that something would have to give. I was worried it would be my sanity or my marriage. I wanted to keep both. Fortunately, an escape clause presented itself.

"I have no idea what to get my husband for his birthday," I told Con. "It needs to be something really special because he's been working his ass off—"

"Ooh, you didn't tell me he was a hustler," Con joked.

I grinned. "I guess I could have chosen my words better, but he's been a good provider and we're getting ready to start a family. This will probably be the last time alone together before the kids begin arriving. I'd like to do something special but something that's not too expensive. But what?"

"Easy, lovey. Give him what he wants most in the world. It's cheap, it'll give you both lots of pleasure, and I'm sure neither of you will ever forget it."

I was puzzled. "What?"

"Indulge his fantasy. Fuck another man in front of him."

I opened my mouth to dismiss the idea, then closed it quickly. Con could probably hear the little cogs in my brain working overtime. Bingo! I had a plan. Leith had rung me earlier to tell me he was having a cunt of a time with one of his difficult clients, one that he could ill afford to antagonize so he had to put up with his continual belittling and his incessant complaining. I told him I'd have something nice and relaxing for him when he got home. Of course, he wanted to know what I had in mind but I was not foolish enough to tell him.

By the time he opened the front door that night, I lay naked on the lounge, my legs spread wide, a movie in which a cute blonde – just the sort he likes – being done over by three muscular studs. It was my favorite and I'd used it many times to get myself off solo while imagining I was the center of attention. The pièce de résistance was that I had my vibrator embedded in my ass.

When I heard his key in the lock, I groaned pretending that I was so turned on I hadn't heard him. Plunging the vibrator in and out of my tight ass which I'd been practicing on all afternoon in order to make this work, I was yelling at the action on the TV, "Fuck me, guys, fuck me hard. Fuck me in the ass and in my dripping cunt. Make me your slut."

Yeah, I know it could have all ended up in total embarrassment but I had my fingers crossed. Plus I had never known Leith to resist my moist cunt when it was on offer. It was the one constant in our lives.

Through half-closed eyes I saw him hesitate in the doorway to the living room as I upped the performance level, hoping he would say something to break the tension.

"So this is what you do while your husband is at work all day?"

I acted surprised and guilty that I had been caught. I attempted to sound flustered. "I wasn't expecting you for ages."

"Obviously."

I noticed the bulge in the front of his trousers and knew the first part of my plan had worked.

"I'm so sorry, honey," I said. "I was just getting myself prepped for your birthday surprise."

He smirked. "My very own floorshow."

I hadn't moved from my position on the lounge. "I was going to let you fuck me in the ass again like you always wanted."

His eyes lit up. "Really? Shit. I had to go and spoil it. Maybe I could go back outside and come in again, pretend I haven't seen you like this although I must admit it's not a sight I'm going to forget any time soon."

"No, it's spoiled." I played the petulant brat expertly. "You might as well fuck me in the ass now."

He was stripping his office clothes off before I'd finished the sentence. He didn't care whether his surprise was spoiled or not. The foreplay was perfunctory, a quick kiss on the lips before he greased his cock with the Vaseline I'd placed strategically next to me and then he pulled the vibrator from my well-lubricated ass before positioning the head of his cock at my sphincter. He pushed slowly and for all my preparation, it stung. I must have flinched because he said, "Relax, honey. It will only hurt for a little bit."

I wonder how he knows it will only hurt for a little while. Funny what goes through your mind at a moment like that.

He was correct though. Once he'd breached my asshole and slowly inserted his cock all the way in, he remained still for a few seconds until I adjusted to the fullness. It sure felt different to the plastic vibrator and, for a while, I wondered why gay men would put themselves through such agony then the pain subsided and Leith began to move his pelvis embedding his cock deep inside me. "Oh, baby, you're so fuckin' tight," he groaned. "That's it, baby, grip my cock, milk me with your ass muscles."

Once the pleasure took over from the pain, I followed his instructions to the letter, improving my skills and drawing him irrevocably into my scheme. "Fuck me, honey. Fuck my ass. I love the feel of your big hard cock deep inside my ass."

With my verbalization and that from the movie on the flat screen TV there was a frisson of debauchery in the room. Leith picked up pace, pounding my ass like it was the only opportunity he'd ever get but I was wondering whether I was missing out on something here. Fifty million gay men couldn't all be wrong.

Sure, I needed a bit more practice because by the time Leith blew his load up my ass, calling on God to witness how great his orgasm was, I was sore from all the friction. I didn't let on as it was time for the rest of my routine.

"Oh, honey, I'm so sorry I spoiled your birthday surprise."

He was still puffing from the exertion, wiping his cock with tissues and then tending my sore ass. Finally, he slumped on the lounge. He really noticed the porn movie for the first time, a smile playing around his lips. Good.

"Now I'll have to come up with something totally new for your birthday. I've gone and spoiled it all. I'm so sorry."

He put his arm around me but it was so perfunctory I knew his concentration was on the screen. "That's okay, baby," he said without even turning to look at me, "That was present enough. It made my day."

"But I want your birthday to be special. Really special."

The hook was baited but no catch. Try again.

"I wish I could think of something to make your birthday the best you ever had."

Nothing.

This was harder than I thought. Obviously subtlety wasn't going to work.

"I'd do anything to make your birthday dreams come true. Anything."

"Um…really?" He was on autopilot. Then it must have sunk into his brain for he turned and looked at me. "Anything? You really mean that? Anything at all."

Got him!

"To show you how much I love you, I'd do anything."

There was silence for the longest while.

"Is there something you really, really want, honey?" I asked ever so innocently. "Just name it, it's yours."

From the way he was slowly drawing it out he thought he was the spider whereas I knew he was the fly.

"You might think it's too much. You might think I'm a pervert or something."

"No, I won't darling, what is it you'd like?"

"What do you think of the movie?" He was scouting around the subject.

"The porno you mean?"

He nodded.

"It's hot. She's one lucky bitch."

He swallowed hard. "You ever thought of doing something like that?"

"Making a porno?"

"No, making out with more than one guy."

Shocked outrage. "I'm a married woman."

He wasn't going to give up that easily. "In your fantasies?"

I went all coy. "Sometimes."

He was like an eager teenager. "How would you like to make your fantasies come true?"

Now all I had to do was reel him in.

"How could I do that?"

"Like I've been suggesting. You know, let me watch another guy make love to you."

"What? You're suggesting you want to watch three guys make love to me?"

I could tell he was because his cock was rock solid at the thought.

"Or maybe two guys and me."

"You think you could cope with that without getting jealous?"

"Fuck yeah."

"That's what you'd really, really like for your birthday?"

"Fuck yeah."

"Truly? This is not just a test to catch me out or something."

"No, not at all."

It was time to set a few parameters. "It's not an excuse for you to fuck other women because I wouldn't like that."

"Not interested, you're the only woman for me."

"Who did you have in mind for the other men?"

I knew it. He started to mention his mates who often tried it on with me when Leith wasn't around. No way.

"Listen," I interrupted. "I couldn't do it with anyone we know. Too embarrassing. It would have to be with strangers we'd never see again."

He was disappointed his mates weren't about to get their leg over, but still turned on by the fact I was considering it.

"Okay," he agreed reluctantly.

"What if nobody wants me?"

He was amazed. "Are you serious? Lady, you are so fuckin' hot, you'd have them lining up around the block."

Mm, does the ego good to hear something like that every now and then.

I took a deep breath. "I'll tell you what, you take a week off work and book us into a resort somewhere that there's bound to be lots of young good-looking guys and we'll see what happens."

"You sure? I don't want you to do this if it's against your nature," he said with mock concern.

"You changing your mind?"

"No way," he said adamantly.

"Balls in your court," I said. "Now fuck me, I haven't come yet."

If his eagerness to see me nailed by some stranger's dick was in direct proportion to his spending on a holiday resort, then he was eager as hell. He showed me the Paradise Palms Resort website and I fell in love. It was gorgeous. Like my man. My pussy tingled at the thought of a week at this oasis of calm and not a little because of the promised 'dirty weekend' aspect of the trip.

I thought that might tarnish the prospect but I had to be honest with myself, it enhanced it. It was unbelievable how much I was looking forward to a foreign cock in my pussy now. I had not convinced myself of the three into one arithmetical equation yet, but, I'd get there.

We both swore off sex in the days leading up to our short holiday which had the effect of putting us both on edge. I was as jittery as the head on one of those bobble dogs people have in their cars, my sexual urges wound to screaming point. Leith seemed to be in pain from a perpetual erection. It was all I could do to keep my hands, lips and pussy off it. You'll notice I didn't include ass in that list. After a few more turns at back-door sex, I decided it really wasn't for me. Sure, I could grit my teeth and endure it but it wasn't in the same ballpark as the shrieking orgasms Leith produced in my pussy or even the satisfaction I got from hearing my man groan as he shot his load into my mouth.

Sometimes I lay awake at night wondering what had happened to me. I'd suddenly developed a voracious sexual appetite, I was watching more and more porn movies, the toys that I'd relegated to the back of the wardrobe when I married had been brought out, used, and replaced with more modern devices.

Don't get me wrong, I was still capable of a 'normal' life, whatever that is. I worked, I cooked, I bought groceries. But now I looked at the guys in the supermarket differently, eyeing them up as prospective partners. And they knew, because they'd smile a cheeky little lopsided grin that gave the game away. I felt like such a slut even though I'd never contemplate following through. Or I wouldn't have if Leith hadn't been pushing me.

On the way to the airport in the taxi, we both must have realized this was the last opportunity to turn back.

"Are you sure…" we both began simultaneously.

"Are you sure this is what you want?" I asked.

To answer Leith took my hand, placing it on the throbbing bulge in his casual trousers. He looked so hot in his muscle hugging casual short-sleeved shirt, his navy casual slacks and his loafers that I wanted to take him on the back seat in full view of the driver. The way Leith's cock throbbed I think he would have been in it with no qualms at all.

"Very sure," he croaked. "Are you completely sure you want to go through with it?"

I didn't want to appear as eager as I felt. "Let's just play it by ear." When I saw the look of hurt on his face, I added, "But I'm keen to try."

The driver caught my eye in his mirror.

"Where are you folk off to? Somewhere sunny by the looks of it."

Leith told him the name of the resort and the cabbie whistled. "Nice."

"We hope so," I said.

"You after a bit of surf, sun, and…" He let the final word hang.

"Yeah, all the above," I joked.

"From what I hear from passengers coming back from a holiday there you'll get all that and a lot more. If you know what I mean." He tapped the side of his nose, winking at me in the mirror.

That made me appraise him more carefully. I estimated he was in his mid-to-late forties but hadn't gone to seed like so many cabbies whose sedentary work practices led to a fat ass and a blubbery waist line. I couldn't see a lot of him, but from the chest up I'd give him a seven and a half or maybe an eight. I needed to clean out my brain, I was doing that mark out of ten routine all the time now. It wasn't like Leith had given me permission to fuck with everyone who scored an aggregate of 8.3 or more. Still, it wouldn't hurt to check out the rest of his body when we got out of the taxi.

The cabbie kept up his mildly suggestive banter the rest of the journey, making my pussy drip so that I thought with all my wriggling I'd stain the seat which, in turn, because he knew what was happening, sent Leith into short breathing spasms that sounded as if a heart attack was imminent. I knew that sound so I was not concerned for his health but for his trousers if he blew a load prematurely.

The melee at the airport splashed a dose of reality in our faces but not until I got a good look at our driver whose mark went up to 8.5 once I saw his tight body and the obscene bulge in his company trousers. My husband was off getting a trolley for our luggage as I helped the cabbie unload our baggage.

"That little mishap on the back seat…" I whispered, rushing to apologize. "I'm so sorry; I'll pay to have it cleaned."

"Fuck, lady, that's what vinyl seat covering was made for. It will be a pleasure to, you know…"

I didn't, but the way he stuck out his tongue as if lapping up a saucer of milk – I almost lost total control.

I couldn't believe what I said next. "Pity, wish I'd known, I could have left more than just a taste on the seat."

He cocked his head in Leith's direction. "What about hubby?"

"Let's just say, he's the adventurous type."

The cabbie fumbled in his pocket, extracting his card which he thrust into my hand eagerly. "Listen lady…"

"Hazel."

"Matches your eyes," he continued. "If you ever need a very special taxi for anything, call the number, day or night."

I smiled mischievously. "And if I'm with hubby?"

"For someone as hot as you, Hazel, I don't mind sharing. I don't mind an audience. I think I read the situation right."

I glanced at the card. "Yes, you did, Matt."

Leith was back by this time, loading the trolley with our luggage, his raised eyebrow all I needed to let me know he was on to my game. Once we were inside the terminal, pushing through the crowds, my mind snapped to a vision of Matt, his long tongue lapping the cab seat to hoover up all my dried juices. I let out a little squeak.

Leith laughed. "I saw the effect you had on that poor driver. Now, what were you saying about nobody wanting you?"

The check-in was automated, our luggage was carry-on, the flight was smooth, joining the Mile-High Club a non-event because we'd sworn to 'save' ourselves, and two hours later we were awaiting our transfer to the resort. It was a little off the beaten track so for the price of accommodation they threw in a limo to take customers to and from the airport. It was the exclusivity of the Paradise Palms that attracted jetsetters from all over the world including many on the celebrity A-list. My wish was that Colin Farrell or some other big, in all senses of the word, star would help out with indulging Leith's fantasy.

I can dream, can't I?

Suddenly everywhere I looked there were hot men, including Pablo, our extremely handsome and extremely personable young limo driver whose all-white uniform, black was too hot in the tropical heat, was designed to excite. I was amused that what excited young Pablo was not me, but Leith, who was blithely unaware of the effect he was having on our driver.

I nudged Leith, nodding at the obvious erection bulging against the limo driver's trousers. Hubby, of course, immediately misinterpreted my meaning.

"You want him?"

"No, you ass, you did that?"

He couldn't have been more surprised. "He's gay?"

I nodded, watching Leith for any flicker of interest in the driver. He looked him up and down but as if examining him rather than appraising him as a potential conquest. "Nah," he said, and that was case closed.

By the time we reached the actual resort, Leith was squirming uncomfortably in his seat as Pablo turned the full force of his personality on flirting with my husband while I sat ignored but smiling superiorly sipping a vodka and lime from the limo bar. Leith had settled on a beer in a vain effort to proclaim his hetero proclivities. I thought Pablo's behavior was borderline harassment especially as Leith looked patently uncomfortable.

The vista as we swept down the coast road was breath-taking and my heart skipped a beat at spending time in such a luscious tropical paradise. In the distance we could see the resort which stood prominently on the headland then hugged its way around the edge of a small bay like a dragon and its tail.

"Welcome to Paradise Palms," Pablo said expansively, reminding me of that old television program, *Fantasy Island.*

I wondered what the story writers would have done with our fantasy. Problem with TV, you can always manufacture a happy ending; real life is very different. Our arrival up the ochre-colored gravel driveway to the front double glass doors of the impressive hotel foyer dispelled any lingering doubts I might have had. Even Pablo's blatant proposition, "If there's anything Pablo can do for you, sir, anything at all, just ring the front desk and I'll be yours to command," while pointedly ignoring me, didn't dampen my enthusiasm.

It wasn't worth complaining as it would get the holiday off to a bad start, so I laughed it off.

"I think you might be right about that Pablo guy," Leith grizzled as we marched into the foyer to register. "But 'yours to command.' Hmm. I like that idea." He was grinning.

"Don't even try that on me, buster," I replied.

"Damn."

"Feel free to try your masterly command on Pablo any time," I joked.

"You didn't fancy him?" Leith asked.

I stopped mid-stride to ask. "Are you going to try to pair me up with every man we run into? That will get boring real quick. I'll let you know when we meet the 'right one.' Okay?"

He looked sheepish for a moment, then pursued his original line of questioning. "You haven't answered my question about Pablo."

"Yes, he's hot," I admitted. "He's also pushy, not interested in me, and very, very gay."

"But if he wasn't?"

"He's a nine out of ten," I said after considering carefully. Pablo was definitely fuckworthy. He simply wasn't interested.

"What am I?" Leith asked mischievously.

"You're my husband."

He sulked.

"You're an eleven. And there can be only one eleven in my life. Got it?"

"Gotcha."

We got to the front counter staffed by a young man whose beauty rivaled that of the opulent marble foyer which would not have looked out of place as part of the Taj Mahal. He had ogled Leith all the while we walked along the plush red carpet to meet his panic-stricken amazement when he saw me up close.

"I'm sorry," he hiccupped obsequiously, "but we are totally booked out."

Leith, oblivious to everything as usual, replied, "That's okay, we have a booking," handing over the paperwork he'd printed from the computer.

Mr. Lennard, as the man's identification badge proclaimed him to be, forensically examined the print-out as if sniffing out a forgery. When he couldn't fault it, he turned to his computer for help, expelling a small yelp of surprise when he discovered we were, in fact, legit. He examined me with the same forensic disdain that he'd used on the booking sheet, sniffed, and then leaned forward as if to impart a shameful secret.

"There has obviously been some mistake. I'm really sorry, but you can't stay here."

That got my back up.

"Why's that?" Leith asked politely.

"It's our fault, sir. But this is Pride Week at Paradise Palms."

"Oh," Leith prided himself on catching on quickly. "That's why all the flags."

I caught on more quickly. The flags were all rainbow colored. I now knew what that meant, thanks to Con at the sex shop. Leith obviously didn't have a clue.

I interrupted. "Not a problem."

"You know what the flags mean?" the receptionist sneered.

He needed a good slap across the chops but that wouldn't get us our room key. My face broke out in the widest smile ever although when I caught a glimpse of myself in the mirror along the wall behind the front desk it looked more like I was having an attack of hives than a grin. "We're very gay friendly," I proclaimed. Leith looked startled by that admission and then somewhat troubled as it sank into his brain. He obviously saw his fantasy week collapsing before his eyes.

"Oh, look, I'm so sorry. Silly me. I was supposed to tell you we're staying here with friends, Bobby and Johnny."

It was a spur-of-the-moment lie but the look of surprise on Mr. Lennard's face revealed I'd struck pay dirt.

He had us sign the registry, had whipped out the keys, and signaled the bellboys with such alacrity I thought someone had plugged him into the power. The change was miraculous.

"I'm so sorry for the misunderstanding when you first arrived*," he bowed so low I thought he'd bump his head on the counter.

*Translation: "I was a total asshole when you first arrived but, please, I can't afford to lose my job."

I wasn't here to antagonize anyone so I took the blame. "That's all right, Mr. Lennard—"

"Please. Please, call me Bruce."

"Why, thank you, Bruce. The misunderstanding was entirely my fault. I'll be sure to let your employer know that you handled what could have been a very unfortunate incident in a most generous and professional manner."

Snap!

"I'd be most grateful, Mrs. —"

"Do call me, Hazel. This is my husband, Leith."

Leith was utterly confused but shook hands with Bruce although the handshake went on just a second or two longer than necessary. I'd have to watch my man this week or he'd run off with some fancy gay boy. Pablo, for instance. I wondered whether Leith had a few more fantasies tucked away in his underpants. Domination fantasies, for example.

I could see he was eager for an explanation but we waited until the two bellboys had escorted us to our bungalow with a view out across the bay, after Bruce had whispered instructions in their ears and suddenly I was treated like the lady I wasn't. Bobby and Johnny were apparently very big cogs in the wheel and needed to be oiled constantly.

Once we had been shown the air conditioning switches, how to cue the hot and cold water in the bathroom shower, and given a simplistic road test of the complicated remote control for the flat screen attached to the wall, we were left to ourselves.

"Okay, please explain all that to me. Who are Bobby and Johnny? And does Pride week mean that my birthday is going to be all glitter and disco and no substance?"

"Well, it sure looks as if this week has been turned over to a gay clientele," I said.

Leith looked deflated, so I added, "But look on the bright side. You can always phone Pablo and order him around a bit." I didn't like the look of pleasure he got from the thought of that.

How could I make what threatened to become a total disaster into something memorable for him. Did I care if he ordered Pablo about a bit? Not really. Did I care if Pablo sucked my husband's dick? The idea turned me on, as long as I was watching. Ah, now I was beginning to understand Leith's fantasy.

"Why don't we pack it in here?" Leith said. "Hire a car and head off up the coast, see if we can find another place to stay that might be more...um..."

"No way. I love it here and we've hardly even scratched the surface yet. I intend to enjoy myself. I suggest you do the same."

"I don't suppose Bobby and Johnny are two guys you organized to...you know?"

"Afraid not. I happened to glimpse a pretty impressive letter near Bruce's computer, signed with those two names. It was also stamped with VIP in big red letters so I took a chance."

Leith kissed me on the forehead. "Smart woman."

"So we can have a relaxing week of sun, surf and, what's that other S word. I know, sex. Okay, it might have to be with me alone, but that's still fun, isn't it?"

"Sure is, honey," he replied, although his cock stayed limp in his pants. "But you'll still be willing to try what we talked about when we get home?"

"Tell you what. We'll take any chance that comes along. How's that? Every opportunity that presents itself, we'll treat as a new adventure." His cock was hardening, so on I plunged. "Anything that happens here, stays here. It won't impinge on our relationship in any way. Besides, one of these gay guys is bound to be bi."

"I'd prefer a straight guy. This is all about me watching you."

"Just maybe I might like to watch you," I chuckled. "With another man."

He'd obviously never thought of that. I'd let him stew over it for a while because I knew him well enough that his brain would automatically focus on the idea as what he'd have to give me for my next birthday.

We unpacked the few items we'd brought along and then headed to one of the three restaurants for lunch. Word had obviously spread like a brush fire because as soon as we announced our bungalow number and names to the maître d' we were shown to a table beside a huge glass window that overlooked the bay and down onto the beach below. The waiters were so attentive I felt like royalty.

"I sure hope Bobby and Johnny don't find out about us before we leave."

"What, honey?" Leith hadn't been paying any attention.

I followed his line of sight. Fuckin' Pablo delivering another load of guests. Leaning across the table, I attempted to imitate Pablo's accent, "I want to be your slave."

Leith coughed to cover his embarrassment.

We had a light lunch with a popular, but expensive, chilled white wine so that by the time we'd finished our meal I was merry. It was mid-afternoon when we left the restaurant and I pleased the maître d' by complimenting him on his staff, asking also that my compliments be conveyed to the chef on his culinary skills. I also insisted that Leith leave a larger than average tip to ensure we got similar service next time.

I was eager to set out exploring but Leith, who had been up hours earlier than me in preparation for our journey, decided a nap was in order. I pored over the maps of the resort which certainly had just enough of interest to keep me occupied for a week; that was before I discovered the extra Pride Week calendar. That was more like it. It proved beyond any shadow of a doubt that gay men really know how to par-tay!

Just looking at a map dotted with 'clothing optional,' 'beware bodies in the undergrowth,' and 'for the broad of mind only' got my pussy buzzing. What fascinated me most was the shaded area with a large red cross inside a circle, labeled with 'Don't say you weren't warned.'

I considered myself warned, however, I was intrigued. As I've always seen myself as a broad-minded woman, 'X' marked the spot. I'd start there. It was hot even this late in the afternoon and outside the air-conditioned comfort of the bungalow I'd been perspiring badly. I slipped into my bikini which I'd chosen because it showed off my assets to my advantage. What a waste. Just when the men are so hot you want to be molested, you end up at a gay resort.

I knew better than to wake Leith, so I wrote a note telling him where I was headed and to come catch up when he awoke. I thought I might stumble across a couple of gay guys holding hands, kissing that sort of thing – that would be hot enough to get my juices flowing, enough to show my husband a good time for bringing me here. Maybe I'd even let him fuck my ass. I screwed my face up even as I contemplated it.

I followed the map, the lay-out was not at all difficult to grasp, passing any number of handsome men with chiseled bodies who nodded and smiled as they passed me. I wondered whether you had to reach a certain level of perfection before you were allowed to be gay, that's how appealing these men were. By the time I reached the grotto, my bikini was doing little to disguise my arousal, the crotch damp with my cunt juice.

The grotto turned out to be an area of meandering paths beneath a canopy of trees and twisted vines that filtered out most of the light so the area was dim and shadowy, easy to disappear into bushes and gardens. I heard movement among the plants that were obviously grown for cover, but also low moaning and the occasional burst of profanity. If I thought everyone would take advantage of the camouflage, I was mistaken. The paths meandered so that it was impossible to see what lay around the next curve or large bush, sometimes startling me when I almost ran into a couple openly kissing or groping. At first I mumbled an apology for intruding until I noticed passing men did no such thing, sometimes taking an opportunity to join in with those indulging in sex play. It was all so casual.

Eventually all those twists and turns took me deeper into the grove and I became lost. The map was little help here, and there were fewer people to ask direction. In fact, I hadn't passed anyone in ten minutes or more. As I rounded a rather abrupt curve in the path I surprised two men fucking on one of the many wooden benches dotting the grotto. I was out in the open before I even saw them, otherwise I probably would have remained in shadow and watched. I didn't know where to look or what to say. The vision of the guy on top ramming his rather substantial cock into the younger and slimmer guy's ass did things to my pussy and I shuddered as I felt the beginnings of orgasm wracking my body. I could do little but stand and gape openly while my body shuddered.

It was all very well watching video porn but the real thing was so much better, except for the fact there were no close-up shots of penetration. The two men saw me but rather than abusing me for my blatant voyeurism they smiled with a sort of dreamy satisfaction.

"Come closer if you want to watch," the younger man whispered without breaking the mood.

I couldn't help myself and stumbled forward to get as close as I could. I was so horny I wanted Leith to get here quickly to fuck me into the ground in front of these two gay lovers. It was impossible to wait so I pushed my hand down the front of my bikini until I found my moist cunt, rubbing my clit before sinking a finger into my juicy hole. I couldn't help but groan.

I was unable to take my eyes off the young man's elastic ass lips expanding and contracting as the cock pushed in and out, wishing I had Leith's cock inside me, bringing me to the most exquisite orgasm ever.

"Take your bikini off," the dominant man said. "Let us see your body."

"Don't be frightened," his young partner added. "We like people watching us. It makes us feel good."

My bikini bottoms hit the ground and I stepped out of them. I didn't care what anyone who came along thought of me, after all we were all out looking for the same thing.

"Show us your tits," one of them said so softly I couldn't tell which it was.

I was soon standing totally naked in front of two gay boys fucking on a bench while I fingered my cunt. I had never felt so on fire.

I was so close to the men the older reached over and squeezed my nipple. "You have beautiful tits," he said. "I bet your cunt is really tight."

Oh God, what was I doing?

Arms enveloped me from behind, squeezing my tits and fondling my nipples as the two boys concentrated now on their own pleasure seeing that Leith had finally caught up.

"She's been waiting for you," the young man said as he watched Leith replace my finger with his own, frigging me with more power and urgency. The advantage of a husband is he knows what turns you on. He licked my ears and bit the back of my neck, one of my most sensitive areas.

His fingers were doing the trick and suddenly my pussy spasmed trapping his hand as I shuddered like a mad woman, my eyes closing, my mouth opening in a low moan. While I was still in the throes of pleasure, Leith bent me forward so my face was level with the two men and I had to grab the edge of the bench to stop from being pitched forward. My husband's cock found my dripping cunt and pushed home.

"Oh fuck," I sighed, wishing I could scream my excitement to the heavens. I knew it would be a short-lived fuck because we were both so on edge sexually from having remained celibate for a week and from the teasing of the past few days that Leith would have the shortest fuse on record. He still managed to give my cunt quite a battering, panting as he held my hips tightly, the two gay boys attempting to match our rhythm. I watched them and they watched us, it was the most erotic thing I had ever done. I'd never been a voyeur until Sue introduced me to the porn movies and I would never have imagined I was an exhibitionist.

"Fuck her hard," the young man called to my husband. "Make her come again."

Leith obeyed like it was an official command and fucked me harder until I thought my knees would buckle. I loved the feeling of being screwed in public while two men fucked just as savagely in front of us. There was a sexual camaraderie at work here and we were feeding off one another's need.

"Oh, shit. I'm gonna come," the young man cried out.

The older man looked at Leith. "Make her suck him. Make her take the little gay pig's cum in her mouth. He's never had a woman's lips around his cock before."

"No," the boy cried, but he was too far gone to do anything about it. The older man pulled my head toward the hard cock that was oozing pre-cum over his belly. He rubbed my face in it before I could get my tongue to lick it up, then pushed me toward his boyfriend's rock hard prick until I felt it in my mouth. I had never sucked another man's cock since I'd married Leith. My mouth was full of hot man cock and I was sucking, dear God, I was sucking it as my cunt exploded, my spasms catching Leith by surprise so that the extra pussy grip provoked his own orgasm and he shot bolt after bolt deep inside me.

My young man squirted, his cum coating my tongue, dribbling down my throat until I was forced to swallow it all or choke. Fuck it was sweet. Finally, the older man groaned as his fucking became short, sharp jabs at his partner's ass as he obviously lost his load.

Slumping forward I landed on my knees, Leith's cock slipping from my slimy cunt as the young man's prick popped from my mouth. I was dizzy so I put my head against the cold wood to steady myself. I'm not sure how long I remained like that but when I looked up, I was alone.

I felt sperm ooze down my leg, my face was sticky with drying cum and my mouth was full of cock phlegm. I grabbed my bikini and ran. There were two explanations, only two. Leith was so repulsed by what I'd done by sucking off another man he'd run away to hide his embarrassment and/or jealousy. Much more likely was that the man who'd just fucked me was not Leith at all. I'd been so horny I'd just accepted that because we were at a gay resort, no one would find a woman attractive enough to fuck. How wrong I'd been.

Panting, I stopped to dress before I ran into other people on the pathway, and then ran for my life. If I could get back to the bungalow before Leith was likely to wake up, I could have a shower and pretend the whole thing never happened.

Alas, the plans of mice and women…

I burst into the bungalow to find him sitting on the bed reading my note.

"Sorry, babe," he said. "I was fucked. I needed that sleep."

He looked at me before I had a chance to escape.

"What have you been up to? You look all flustered."

"Nothing much," I lied.

"Maybe you're just super horny like I am," he grinned.

"I think I'll take a shower to freshen up."

He grabbed my wrist, pulling me onto the bed. "Come here, babe. The shower can wait."

Please God, don't let him kiss me.

His mouth went to my face and in turning away his lips brushed the patches of dried spunk on my nose and cheek. He ran his tongue along his lips to taste the foreign matter he'd found. He arched his eyebrows and then went for my mouth, flicking his tongue across mine and around my gums as if taste testing.

There was nothing I could do. I just prayed that he wouldn't ask because I couldn't lie to him. He ran his hand over my stomach and I tried to hold his hand away from my steaming pussy but it was no use. His finger dipped into my hole, sloppy with my own juices and with the sperm of some stranger I didn't even see. Leith wrenched my bikini bottoms off me and parted my legs, slipping down the bed until he stared at my glistening pussy.

"Mmmm, you know how much I love to eat your pussy, Hazel, suck all your juices out of you."

"I wouldn't today, Leith. Please," I begged.

My warning went unheeded and he attached his mouth to my cunt like a leech, licking my clit and sucking the mixed spunk out, swallowing another man's cock snot. He would never forgive me. For a while as another orgasm clenched my belly I didn't care but then Leith was kneeling over me, his mouth shiny with cock and cunt slime.

"Who was he?" he asked.

"Oh, honey, I'm so sorry. Please forgive me. I thought he was you," I sobbed.

"Okay," he said. "Stop blubbering. Tell me all about it. Slowly and in great detail. I'm not angry, love, except that I wasn't there to see it. Now tell me everything. Don't skimp on the detail."

As I began my story, he slipped his cock into my pussy and gently fucked me until the end of my sorry tale at which point he banged me so hard I thought the bed would collapse. When he shot his load it was so powerful I swear I felt every individual sperm shatter against my cunt wall.

He collapsed on the bed beside me and then gathered me in his arms, showering my face with kisses. "Did you enjoy it?" he asked.

"I was so hot watching the two guys fucking, anyone could have taken me there and then."

"Sounds like they did," he joked.

"Don't," I said. "I didn't mean to cheat on you."

"It wasn't exactly cheating. I gave you permission. Okay, it would have been less like cheating if I'd been there to watch but you told me all about it, that's the next best thing to being there."

"I guess," I sniffled.

"So watching gay guys gets you hot?"

"As Hades."

He chuckled as he held me in a headlock. "Maybe this holiday won't be a write-off after all."

How wrong he was. That first day was the exception rather than the rule. The next day Leith and I went everywhere together, he wanted to be there if it happened again, but the gay guys all came on to him, giving me a wide berth as if I were made from poison ivy. There was no comfort even when we penetrated well into the grotto. Things didn't improve on the third day either and we were getting snappy with each other. Our fucking since that initial explosive coupling as I described my ordeal was lackluster and half-hearted. He was obviously pining for his fantasy and now that I was surrounded by so many semi-naked dream boys I was desperate to grant him his birthday wish. Neither of us knew how to go about it.

After one particularly nasty argument over something so trivial I'd forgotten what it was seconds after we'd begun sniping at each other, I challenged him. "If it's so bloody important to you, why don't you put your ass to good use and wiggle it about in your Speedos to lure some gay boy in to fuck me while you watch. He won't care who he fucks if you get him horny enough."

We both turned our backs on each other in the bed and went to sleep. The following morning his mood was quite chipper. Breakfast helped thaw our relationship further until he asked, "Did you mean what you said last night?"

I knew he wouldn't be asking about the nasty accusation I flung at him. "You mean about luring some poor gay boy into our web?"

"I thought about it last night, it's not a bad idea."

"You're going to become a prick tease?"

"If it gets us both what we want."

I shrugged. I didn't really believe it would work but what the hell? It was better than fighting.

"How do we work this?"

"Well, you hide in the closet. It's got louvered slats that you can position so you can see the bed. I'll get some hot stud here and you can pop out and take care of him while I watch."

My reply was sarcastic. "Yeah, I like the beginning and the end but the middle part needs a little work. Plus I don't like the idea of forcing somebody against their will."

"Simple," he said. "If a guy really isn't interested, his cock won't be hard. Right?"

There was a simple logic to that but I knew some gay men were not at all interested in women while many others were farther along the Kinsey scale and perhaps would be up for a bisexual romp.

"Okay, count me in."

We started the day by parading around the resort in our swimwear. Leith's Speedos hugged his tackle and his solid ass so that he got admiring whistles and stares everywhere we went, especially after we took to the pool and his swimming costume wet was even clingier than it was dry. I managed to lose the top of my bikini so my tits were on open show. Leith wasn't the only one to get lascivious stares after that, although I could have done without the snide queens who passed us and whispered things like, "Do you think they're real?"

Only later did I discover that some men at Paradise Palms believed I was a post-operative cut'n'tuck. Leith laughed so hard I had to hit him to stop. "Besides," I gloated, "The men think you're gay."

I thought that would upset him, but all he did was turn to look at his ass in the mirror and smirk, "Oops, I didn't know it was showing." Then he filled my hot pussy with his ball juice to prove how wrong everyone was about his hetero bona fides.

I was beginning to think this holiday was not such a good idea. Leith was becoming more desperate as his birthday approached and I was so horny all the time I'd shag a palm tree if I could. On top of that I was getting these disloyal thoughts I wished Leith was gay or, preferably, bisexual so I could watch him with the other hot men who so flagrantly threw themselves at him. I was envious, I admit it. The only thing that had prevented my becoming a total slut for the duration was the unavailability of cock because it was gay.

We did our best to parade ourselves as available but while the natives were friendly, no one invited us to play. There were the whispered invitations to Leith if he'd 'ditch the bitch' but he declined. I wondered what would happen if I wasn't with him.

After lunch we returned to our bungalow, noticing for the first time that many of the doors were wide open.

"Aren't they afraid of robbery?" Leith asked.

"Maybe gay boys are more honest," I said.

Leith smiled. "Maybe gay boys are just more honest about what they want. Look." He pointed a short way ahead.

On the edge of the pathway, a young man was casually milking his cock as he stared into an open bungalow. As we drew near we saw another man flat on his back on the bed fingering his ass. In the time it took for us to pass they'd become a couple, leaving the door wide open for voyeurs to watch the action or else join them.

"God, it would be so much simpler being gay," Leith said.

I was feeling snappy. "Why don't you get your good mate, Pablo? I'm sure he'd oblige."

We didn't speak the remainder of the way back. Leith threw himself face down on the bed to show his displeasure at my mood while I fumed and stomped about. It was up to me to apologize in the best way I knew how: spreading my pussy. I stripped off, fingering myself in front of him, pinching my nipples with my free hand. There was no reaction. Thinking I must have really pissed him off, I tried harder to interest his sluggish libido. No dice. Then I heard a sort of a snore. The fucker was asleep. He'd obviously eaten too much or had too much wine with lunch.

I shoved him. Nothing. He wasn't playing, he was out to it. Fucker. How dare he not be awake to fuck me for being sorry. That's how wound up and cranky I was. I decided a swim in the bay might cool me down and bring me to my senses. My second swimsuit was less revealing than my bikini but who did I have to look my best for? I grabbed a beach towel, courtesy of the resort, and headed out, intending to slam the door but the evil bitch inside me thought better of it. It was her that persuaded me to spread Leith's legs apart and position him so his butt, clad in tight shorts, faced the door. The door I left open as I flounced out in high dudgeon.

Had I thought through my actions I probably wouldn't have done it as it could lead to all sorts of complications, or even violence if someone took the view of Leith's ass at face value and tried it on with my husband. Nevertheless, I wasn't going to back down. I was seething. Our lives were in such a mess. I blamed Leith for his obsession with wanting to see me fucked by another man or group of men, and with Sue for introducing me to the stimulating world of gay pornos. That's as far as my blame went. There was no way I was going to think about my lack of self-control at the moment. That would mean part of the responsibility for the problems would be sheeted home to me. No way.

These thoughts were rattling around in my brain regardless of my attempts to censor them when I passed by the bungalow where Leith and I had earlier witnessed brazen exhibitionism. The door was still wide open and the room was a hive of activity, a group of men buzzing around two queens on the bed who were doing their best to accommodate one and all via their various orifices. Swim vs. Peeking. Swim? Peek? You can guess which won.

I stood outside behind a bush near the doorway. The camouflage was to protect me from people on the pathway, not the men inside the bungalow. If they looked up, they'd have an uninterrupted view of me with my fingers embedded in my cunt. It was so unfair, all these randy hot men, me with permission from my husband to enjoy myself, and not a snowball's chance in hell of consummation. Oh well, at least I can watch.

That opportunity was lost as well when one of the men inside saw me voyeuring and closed the door in my face.

That was it! I'd had enough. I was angry, screaming 'Fuck you!' to the men inside even though I was the interloper, to my husband who got me into this situation, to Sue for encouraging me, to the world at large, and to myself for being such a pussy.

Striding back down the path to our bungalow, I would insist on packing up and leaving this sexual madhouse immediately. We'd hire a car, find some nice, respectable resort with real people who didn't think with their genitals all the time. People like…Shit! I was running away from people like me. I wanted to cry. I was going cock crazy. There were so many beautiful men and I wasn't getting any.

Compounding my frustration and anger was Leith lying totally naked face down on the bed when I arrived back. Someone had removed his underwear. His back and ass cheeks were splattered with what suspiciously looked like shiny snail trails. Far too many for just one man. Did they…?

I prized open his butt cheeks to look at his tight puckered hole.

"Mmmm," Leith wriggled. "Lick my ass again, honey. Felt so good. Put your finger in, babe, like you did before. Make me come again."

On top of everything else, I'd missed seeing my man playing the slut for other men. Could this day get any worse?

And then Pablo turned up.

He knocked politely before entering. Leith rolled over to see who it was, revealing his semi-hard prick bathed in his own cum from where he'd ejaculated while someone licked his ass or fingered him. It was no excuse he thought it was me. Plus, there was no excuse he made no effort to cover himself up in the presence of a man who couldn't take his eyes off Leith's tackle while purporting to talk to me.

"Sorry to interrupt but I've been sent to invite you to a private party this evening at Bobby and Johnny's. It seems you know them and they'd love to get reacquainted."

"That's very kind of them," I replied with too much anger to my voice, "But I'm afraid we'll be leaving just as soon as we're packed."

Both Leith and Pablo looked at me first for the first time since my return.

"That won't be possible," Pablo said.

"Oh, I definitely think it will," I said with the air of superiority that comes with determination.

Pablo seemed to be over listening to me. "I don't think Bobby and Johnny will be pleased but I'll let them know."

"Get it through that thick skull of yours, Pablo," I was getting really offensive now. "I don't know these two gay boys. I made it all up to get a booking. I don't even know who the fuck they are."

Pablo smirked. "If they want to meet you, then meet you they will. Main foyer. Nine o'clock. Smart casual."

With one last ogle of my gorgeous naked husband whose cock had hardened considerably during our verbal exchange, Pablo left.

Leith was off the bed, enfolding me in his powerful arms, making me loved and secure but also making me feel like a child.

"What's the matter, honey?" he cooed. "I thought you liked it here."

"Nothing's gone right since the day we arrived," I sobbed. "And it's your birthday tomorrow. It's a bloody disaster."

"Come on, babe. You had a bit of fun the other day watching those gay boys while some stranger's cock got to feel how hot your pussy is."

"Yeah," I mumbled.

"The food is great, the facilities are top notch."

"I guess."

Leith led me to the bed and I'd soon forgotten all my woes as he glued his mouth to my cunt, lapping my juices as he made me orgasm twice. Maybe I had over-reacted. My husband's tongue tamed me.

We turned up in the foyer a few minutes early but Pablo was already waiting.

"I told them you may not show," Pablo said, appraising me this time as much as Leith.

"We don't like to disappoint," my husband responded.

"You won't," he said. "Either of you."

I was pleased we passed muster. Leith looked hot in his tight-fitting casual trousers that showed off his sculpted ass and his thick cock, while I wore a simple black cocktail frock that barely covered my ass, and didn't at all if I bent over, plus a pair of red heels that matched my lipstick. Because the dress clung to my body like a second skin, I went braless and pantyless. We turned heads as we walked across the foyer and I hoped a few of them were for me. I was turned on parading my body near naked even for a gaggle of gay boys. Heaven knows how I would have felt if the men had been straight.

Pablo ushered us to a special elevator that was set apart from the others, a subtle brass plate proclaiming 'Private' attached just above the call button. He needed a key to unlock it and we stepped into a lift that was more luxuriously appointed that our entire home. Leith whistled. As Pablo pressed the only button, I asked, "Who exactly are Bobby and Johnny?"

"They own the resort," he said cheerily. "We're going to the penthouse."

"When you stretch the truth, babe," Leith chuckled, "You sure do it big time."

We were whisked up twenty-five floors in record time, leaving my stomach and my confidence somewhere on ground. I was nervous as hell although it didn't sound as if the two men were at all angry at my ruse. I didn't for a minute entertain the idea they'd sell us both into white slavery.

When the lift pinged that we'd arrived, nothing could have prepared me for the luxury. While it was obvious that a great deal of money had been spent on the furnishings of an apartment that had high glass walls looking out over the bay and the ocean, it was tasteful and subdued. The wealth didn't scream the conspicuous consumption so evident amongst the nouveau riche. Not that we moved in those circles. But this wasn't the sort of home that rubbed your face in designer labels. However, it made me feel decidedly under-dressed. Leith, as usual was oblivious to everything, except the cocktail that was on offer from the silver tray held aloft by a gorgeous man with more muscles than Leith, and a package that promised more inches as well. How do I know? For starters, he was wearing little more than sparkling silver briefs and the brightest smile this side of a cosmetic dentist's surgery.

When he turned to guide us to the hosts, I noticed his ass was as round and as solid as Michelangelo's statue of David.

Leith was amused. "See something you like?"

"Why is God so unkind? She's made all the cute men gay?"

"Not all of them."

I clutched his arm in thanks.

There was a murmur of conversation as we approached the living area with its spectacular views which we'd only just glimpsed from the entrance. It was truly magnificent. There was an older gentleman playing jazz on a baby grand as a group of men stood chatting, listening idly to what was a very superior musician who seemed oblivious to the lack of attention being paid to his prowess. I guessed he was either Bobby or Johnny.

A young man who was so good-looking it made my eyes water came to greet us with his hand outstretched. He shook hands with Leith who seemed as struck by his physical beauty as I was, and then he kissed my hand gently making my pussy tingle. I was beginning to wish I'd worn panties. "Told you," Leith whispered, noticing my discomfort.

"I'm Bobby," he said with the slightest French accent. "Properly Robert as in Robair but that's a bit pretentious, don't you think?"

No, as a matter of fact, I thought that was exotic. Who on earth wants to be known as Bobby? It sounds so young and innocent.

"That's Johnny over there," he said, pointing at an equally gorgeous dark Mediterranean man who was deep in conversation with a man in his thirties. "Don't mind him. When he's discussing architecture, he's oblivious to everything, including me." He shrugged as if to say, 'It's a cross I have to bear.' "The man he's talking to is Pierre, one of the most famous architects in France. He's designing the additions we wish to make to our little resort."

When the formalities were over and Bobby had done his best to relax us, he turned his attention to examining Leith and I from head to toe, his gaze so penetrating that I began to feel uncomfortable. After the longest time, he smiled. "So, you are the two people who have caused so many problems for us?" There wasn't an ounce of rancor to his voice.

"We didn't mean to," Leith said, without apology. "We booked a week here for my birthday and no one said anything about it being gay week."

"No, not your fault," Bobby was quick to soothe. "We will be more careful next year. But you are welcome. I hope everything has been to your liking."

I couldn't help myself, blurting out, "I've never seen so many gorgeous men."

"But you have a very handsome husband," Bobby said. "He has caused many problems among the men at the resort. Problems of frustration mainly."

Leith turned the color of beetroot. Bobby noticed.

"Ah, you are not bisexual then?"

I jumped in, lest Leith give offence. "He's never tried."

"Ah, here is Pierre's young partner, Louis."

An impossibly blond young man flounced into the room, wiping his mouth with the back of his hand. The reason followed behind a few seconds later; the bookend naked waiter of the one who'd greeted us at the door. The only difference being that was wearing revealing gold briefs, into which he was attempting to stuff his semi-erection. When he saw me, I could have sworn his cock gave a twitch of welcome. I'd keep my eye out for him.

Louis didn't just flirt, he threw himself at Leith, who merely looked amused at the pretty young thing. I was jealous. Louis was prettier than me, his long blond hair giving his face a slightly feminine touch which the remainder of his body contradicted. He was as muscular as the rest of the small party. These guys must put in serious gym hours.

When Louis kissed my hand, I whispered. "You missed a bit. There's a glob on the side of your nose." Before he could react, I leaned forward and licked the spunk strip from his face.

"You're wicked," Louis smiled. "I think we'll be great friends. How big is your husband's cock?"

"How big is his?" I nodded in the direction of the waiter who noticed we were talking about him.

"Don't ask, don't tell," Louis joshed and then made a measure with his two index fingers which was grotesquely large, but appealing. I must have salivated because he continued, "So, you're a size queen. You'd go ballistic over what Johnny's got between his legs."

I was intrigued, but we were interrupted by our first waiter discreetly tapping a brass gong. "Dinner is served." It looked so comical, the juxtaposition of the formal announcement from a man whose only item of clothing was a scrap of silver fabric which wouldn't make a man's pocket handkerchief.

We were seated around a smaller round table than the monster that filled the dining room at which I counted places for around eighteen diners. The conversation was general, Leith and Louis discovered a love of football although they barracked for very different teams, while Pierre, Bobby and Johnny began by discussing generalities that, just shy of dessert in an incredibly delicious gourmet meal, turned to our stay at Paradise Palms. The questions were of a highly intimate nature but given the week's activities at the resort it was understandable. I kept trying to attract Leith's attention to intervene as I was feeling intimidated because the three men questioning me, although they were gay, had a disastrous effect on my cunt and I was juicing up enough that it was leaking onto the chair because of my lack of panties. Leith was absolute rubbish at helping me out and, had I not known better, I would have thought he was well on his way to fucking Louis. At the very least, allowing him to suck his cock.

Oh God, the thought of it just made my pussy spasm more.

Johnny turned his dark Mediterranean looks on me. "Is something wrong? You're whimpering."

"No, I'm fine," I managed to croak.

The wine flowed freely and because of a certain nervousness, Leith and I had imbibed more than usual. I knew it was affecting me in all the wrong ways. It was making me incredibly hot and horny. If I didn't cool down shortly I'd need to visit the bathroom and take myself in hand just to relieve the tension.

"Let us take a short interlude before the superb dessert the cook has promised. A little relief for our digestion will make it taste even more appetizing. Also, I think we'd all be a lot more comfortable in the living area for our little show. Bring your wine." We all adjourned to the large semi-circular lounge facing a padded raised platform which had replaced the coffee table while we'd been eating. The seating must have been pre-arranged because I was wedged between Pierre and Johnny and Leith was hemmed in by the other two men. There was absolutely no need for the crowding that I could see as the lounge was big enough to accommodate all of us lying prone.

Bobby had taken the opportunity to lower the lights so the room was in comparative darkness except for the bench which was spotlighted like it would be in a theatre. He turned to the guests, "I know most of you do enjoy our little shows and I'm sure Hazel will find tonight's entertainment highly stimulating. If we offend you, Leith, I apologize in advance but we have nothing to offer you. If you are indeed offended or bored then might I suggest you visit that door over there, behind which you will find a small cinema and quite a collection of…uh…more heterosexually oriented material.

The sound of anthemic heavy rock pumped from an unseen sound system as the two waiters strutted into the room dressed in skin tight shorts, their bodies oiled so they shone like gold in the light.

"Wayne and Lucky are our two most popular models. You'll see why in a moment," Bobby whispered.

I thought I could already see why, both of them had bulges that threatened to split their shorts apart at the seam. They went into a clinch which, because of their oily bodies, meant they slipped and slid against each other until their erections were raging inside their shorts.

They gyrated their way around the small group ogling them. Wayne, the waiter who had met us at the door, came over to me, while Lucky headed toward Louis. The waiters' moves consisted mainly of thrusting out their hips encouraging one of us to unzip their fly. Louis had no problem in obliging and soon Lucky was naked sporting the most enormous cock I'd ever seen, a good few inches longer than my husband's. Louis and Bobby stroked it while Leith had a comic look of horror on his face. I watched closely to see if he would touch it but he sat on his hands.

Meanwhile, either Johnny or Pierre had stripped Wayne and his cock was bobbing very close to my face. All I had to do was lean forward a little.

Johnny placed his hands on my tits, attempting to peel down the top of my tube dress. "Don't worry, Hazel, Wayne is a tit man. I'm sure your husband won't mind." Then he raised his voice to attract Leith's attention. "You don't mind, Leith, do you? Wayne here is a tit man. Loves to fuck his cock between luscious breasts like your wife has. You don't mind? You're among friends here."

I saw the smile spread across Leith's face as he noticed what was going on. "You don't need my permission. As long as it's okay with Hazel it's more than all right with me." He attempted to stand up, probably to come over to watch Wayne's tit fuck in close-up, but he was pinned to the lounge by the two men on either side. Lucky leaned in to whisper in Leith's ear. If it was at all possible, Leith's smile got even wider. He watched as Wayne slid his cock between my breasts before pressing them together to form a tit cunt. What he couldn't see because Bobby was blocking the view, was Pierre running his hand along my thigh and up under my skirt. When he felt no resistance from me he went farther and had his finger at my cunt entrance before he realized I was wearing no panties.

"You are a wanton woman, Hazel. Your pussy is so juicy from watching these strong, virile men. I'll bet if your husband was not here you would have your legs spread wide apart so we could all fuck you like the slut you want to be."

I could have just told him that's what Leith wanted but I decided to play along. I wanted to see how far they would go while they thought Leith might object. I guess what I wanted was the semblance of seduction. Pierre's voice was so exotic, so sexy, so fuckin' French I just wanted to grind my pussy into his mouth.

"What about Louis?' I whispered.

"He knows I have needs to fuck a woman from time to time. He does not mind. He likes to watch."

I squeezed the bulge in Pierre's trousers and almost lost the plot. Not only were these men hot, they were sporting hard-ons the equal or better of Leith's. Oh, dear God.

Pierre's fingers pushed inside me and I clenched as he fucked me gently. I was so close I wouldn't last long, my body on edge as Wayne continued to thrust along my cleavage.

I peeked at the reaction on my husband's face but he seemed to be going through a conflict of his own. He was shaking his head at something Lucky was asking. Louis was swallowing Lucky's cock right down to the root. Unbelievable technique, he should give lessons. Lucky pulled out and Louis looked disappointed to lose the throatful. The waiter aimed it at Leith's face but he resisted. Lucky seemed angry or forceful and Louis was joining in, attempting to push Leith forward. Whatever Lucky said, and Louis nodded his head enthusiastically in agreement, did the trick and Leith slowly opened his mouth and took the head of Lucky's prick in his mouth. He must have found it less awful than he thought because he bobbed his head along the shaft a few inches as Louis and Johnny attempted to hide his activity from me.

Too late. I was so turned on watching Leith suck cock in his virginal way, that I lost control, my body shuddering to the most intense orgasm I'd had in years. It was about twenty seconds before I got control of my breathing and my convulsions. Pierre extracted his fingers and sucked my juice from them, humming his satisfaction.

Bobby clapped his hands together to bring a little decorum to the proceedings. "Bring on the sacrifice." I straightened my skirt and Leith looked somewhat embarrassed although he didn't know I'd seen him cocksucking.

"Your husband is bisexual, no?" Pierre asked.

"I'm afraid he's not," I answered.

"That is a great pity."

The two waiters, now fully naked and erect, disappeared from the room. I hoped by 'sacrifice,' Bobby didn't mean we were going to spit roast one of the guests.

As it transpired, I was half right. Wayne and Lucky dragged a struggling Pablo into the room. I guessed it was playacting because Pablo had a smirk on his face as the two waiters pushed him down on the padded bench and he assumed the doggy position without any coaxing. The other two men slapped him around a bit as if he were their bitch. I noticed Leith's interest perk up as they commanded Pablo to do their bidding and he adjusted his crotch a number of times.

Pablo was crying for mercy as Lucky rubbed his monster along his ass crack. Leith grimaced, while my pussy clutched in sympathy as Lucky slid the full length of his cock into Pablo in one smooth action. My ass didn't even want to know about it, threatening to seal itself up if Lucky came anywhere near it. Was I evil wanting to see Leith on the receiving end? Or at least licking it?

There were catcalls from the four gay men seated on the lounge telling Wayne to pound Pablo's mouth. He didn't need much encouragement, pulling Pablo's hair to get him to open up before inserting his far-from-small prick in the unfortunate limo driver's gullet. Pablo groaned half in pain, half in pleasure by the sound of it, spurring Lucky to fuck him harder, to really give it to him, to breed him. Fortunately I'd heard all the X-rated dialogue before in porn movies. Leith watched attentively. I could tell he was turned on, I could read it in his eyes. This was a whole new experience for him: sex as animal fucking, no love involved.

At home, the two of us were much quieter in our lovemaking, tending to exchange endearments, rather than demanding satisfaction. I was panting, desperate to put my fingers to my cunt but too intimidated by the company to do so. I was close to screaming, the men must have been as tense as I was because their trousers were all tented.

The sex show was only a teaser and it was over almost as soon as it began. The fucking was fast and furious and soon the slaps and groans reached a crescendo as first Wayne then Lucky pulled out, squirting their spunk over Pablo's ass and his face. Bobby and Louis scrambled for the man cream, licking it from Pablo's body like it was the elixir of life. I noticed my tongue was inching its way between my lips before I managed to control it.

"Not too much cream, boys," Johnny admonished jovially. "Leave room for dessert."

"What did you think of the little show, Hazel? I hope it did not upset you," Pierre asked.

"It was over much too soon."

"It excited you, no?"

"Very much so."

"What a pity your husband is with you," Johnny sighed. "I am so in need of cunt. It's been so long."

I had to ask. "Bobby doesn't mind?"

"Good God, no," Johnny said. "He knows I have needs, just as he does."

The dessert was delicious gelato which cleansed the palate and invigorated the senses. It seemed everyone was on edge, the testosterone level wound up like an old-fashioned clock. But it didn't look as if the men were willing to attempt anything in front of Leith. If something didn't happen soon, I suspect I would have to start it and I didn't really want to be the instigator.

Under the camouflage of the table, Pierre and Johnny kept rubbing their fingers across my pussy lips during dessert, winding me up until I was so close to coming, then withdrawing, moving their thumbs back to my clit when the threat of orgasm had subsided. It must have been obvious to anyone at the table what was going on but Leith seemed much too occupied in his conversation with Louis.

The waiters cleared the dishes away but Lucky knocked one last spoon onto the floor as he turned to walk away.

"Don't worry, Lucky," Johnny said, dropping to his knees. "I'll get it and bring it out to the kitchen for you."

It had bounced under the table, so Johnny lifted the cloth which reached almost to the floor and disappeared in search of the recalcitrant spoon. I wondered what was taking him so long until I felt his hands on my legs as he pushed his way up under my skirt. I flinched at his initial touch because it was so unexpected but sank down in my chair as I felt his breath along my thigh as he pushed my skirt higher. I wriggled to allow him to push it up over my butt, opening my legs wider.

I gasped when his tongue buried itself in my pussy. Everyone at the table looked at me as I reached under the table to hold Johnny's head against my cunt. Louis, full of mischief, grabbed the edge of the tablecloth and, with a flourish worthy of a top-class magician, whipped it from the glass table revealing my pussy at the mercy of Johnny's lapping tongue. I didn't care anymore. All pretense gone, I screamed, "Eat my cunt. Make me come, you fucker!"

All eyes turned to Leith. They were possibly expecting the worst but he merely beamed that he was finally getting his wish. There was no way on earth I could have denied him with Johnny drinking my cunt juice, the residual smeared all over his lower face. He'd also turned to my husband regardless of my encouragement to keep at it, in case violence was threatened.

Leith put their minds at rest by saying, "Come on, Johnny, she wants it, mate. Eat her fuckin' pussy. She loves it. Give her what she wants."

There was an audible sigh of relief.

"Gentlemen, I think we would be more comfortable if we took this to the living room. And if we got out of our restricting clothes," Bobby said.

They encouraged me to adopt the same position as Pablo had earlier and I obliged gladly. The men sat on the lounge stroking their cocks as Johnny lined his cock up with my dripping pussy. He sank into me and I sighed so deeply I thought I'd pass out from lack of oxygen. This was what I'd been waiting for all week. It was also what Leith had been begging of me for years. I was a dummy to have waited so long. It was so good to feel another man's cock in my pussy. Of course, I still loved my husband but what a joy to be fucked by someone else. I looked over at him and mouthed, "Is this what you want?"

He had the glazed look of a satisfied man and nodded. He was panting more than if he had his cock buried in me himself. He was stroking himself slowly, prolonging the exquisite agony, while Louis and Bobby eyed his luscious meat.

I screamed for Johnny to fuck me hard, visions of Lucky's slab in my mind. Could I take something that big without injuring myself? Leith must have read my mind because he said to Bobby, "Why don't you invite the waiters to join us, I'm sure they'd like a chance to fuck my wife."

"And you're okay with that?" Pierre asked.

I knew Leith well enough to know he wanted to watch me take on Lucky and that's what the two of them had been discussing in secret earlier. I shivered with both horror and anticipation at the prospect but I didn't want Leith to get off scot free.

"I'm okay with anything she wants to do," he said. I was about to add that I'd like to see him with his legs in the air, a man's cock buried deep in his ass so he knew what it's like but he got in before me. "Why don't one of you plug her mouth, kebab the bitch?"

Pierre stepped up to the plate. "It'll be my pleasure."

I was gagged so successfully all I could do was hum around the prick in my mouth as it plunged deep in my throat. I choked a couple of times, grateful now that I'd practiced on Leith's cock so that I'd learned how to control my breathing.

I wondered what Leith was thinking and feeling as he watched his wife of ten years make a slut of herself, admittedly at his instigation. I also wondered how many of the gay men at the party were up to fucking me. I'd already pegged that Bobby wasn't a likely candidate and I doubted that pretty boy, Louis, would be into cunt either. Or Pablo. That still left Wayne, Pierre, Johnny, and the incredible Lucky.

It took a while but eventually I stopped thinking about Leith and what he was doing. I didn't care really, I was having fun of my own and I was sure if something outrageous occurred the action around me would stop so we could watch. He was much too uptight to get involved.

"You want to fuck your wife, Leith?" Pierre asked.

"Nah, mate. I'm happy to sit here and watch. An opportunity like this doesn't come along all that often."

There didn't seem to be any trace of sarcasm or jealousy in his voice. It sounded sluggish with lust, if anything. I was making his fantasy a reality and it seemed to be exactly what he wanted. As long as he was getting his jollies I could relax and enjoy myself. There was a lot of activity around me now as Wayne and Lucky joined the party. Bobby and Louis must have joined their respective partners and I noticed out of the corner of my eye that Louis was kissing Pierre as he shoved his cock down my throat. Behind me I heard Johnny saying, "See, Robert, the way her cunt lips expand and drag against my cock as I pull it out and push it back in. The feeling is so intoxicating. You should try it. There's nothing like a moist cunt unless, of course, it's your tight little asshole, love."

"I love watching you, Johnny. I like to see your big cock wedged in some slut's cunt or asshole. I'm so proud to know you're giving them so much pleasure."

There was a lot more talk like this but I shut it out to concentrate on my own body. I never knew two cocks could feel so wonderful or that having a pair of lips on my nipples while I was being fucked could heighten my arousal, but Wayne had slipped beneath me and suckled like a new-born babe. I paced myself because I didn't want to peak too soon.

Suddenly I felt Pierre pull his cock from my mouth. He hadn't come so I wondered what had happened.

"Go on, babe, put your cock in her mouth. I promise you'll love it." Pierre was encouraging Louis to try hetero sex.

His cock was as cute as he was and almost as big as Leith's. I wanted to show him I was as good at sucking as any gay man but he was reluctant until Pierre began jerking his cock, pushing his body closer to my mouth until, with a little stretching, I wrapped my lips around the tip of his shaft.

Louis gasped and I knew I had him. He relaxed as I took him down my throat putting more effort into his blow job than I did into Pierre's. This was Louis's first female mouth around his delicious cock and I wanted him to remember it. He closed his eyes but I wasn't offended, he could think of whomever he liked, as long as he gave me his ball juice. I sucked and licked and tongued until I felt him tense, his balls clench and he flooded my mouth with his spunk. I kept it on my tongue so that when he finished shooting his load, I opened my mouth for Leith and the others to see.

"So fuckin' nasty," Leith said.

I looked over to ensure he meant it and I noticed Pablo had his hand on my husband's cock manipulating it slowly. Fuck, that was hot. I winked at Pablo and he must have understood because he leaned over and took Leith's cock in his mouth.

My man didn't even flinch, he merely held Pablo's head in place and whispered hoarsely, "That's it, boy, suck my prick. Show me how much of a fag slut you are." I heard the sound of a hand meeting flesh and knew Leith must be spanking Pablo's marbled ass cheeks.

The men surrounding me took turns swapping positions although Lucky held off, joining Leith on the lounge and I could hear them both whispering and plotting. In between men changing orifices I noticed Bobby down on his knees servicing Lucky while Pablo had his mouth around Leith's cock with Louis hovering, anxious to get into the action.

The guys dumped their cum in my cunt, and down my throat while I had three shuddering orgasms that shook the very foundations of my sexual world. My life would never be the same after this holiday. There was no way either of us could turn our backs on what we'd done. Pandora's Box, as well as mine, had been opened. I reveled in cock and cum, wishing that Leith would get more involved.

I needn't have worried because when I stopped to move positions because of cramp, I was delighted to see Leith had his cock buried in Pablo's ass while Bobby buried his prick between the limo driver's lips. What was more exciting, however, was the fact that Louis and Leith were in the throes of a passionate lip-lock. If there was one thing I liked more than seeing my man with his cock buried up some fag ass it was my man with his tongue down another man's throat.

We watched my husband owning up to his gay side, groaning his orgasm as he shot his muck deep inside Pablo's ass. Bobby followed a few moments later, depositing so much cum it dribbled down the side of Pablo's chin.

The silence that followed was awkward until Lucky reminded us, "I haven't come yet. Who wants to volunteer?"

I jumped in quickly. "It's my Leith's birthday, and I want to give him an extra special present, so I'd love to take that cock of yours in my cunt, Lucky. And to make it an occasion that none of us will forget, how about you fuck my ass at the same time, Johnny. And Pierre, would you do the honors with my mouth."

Leith looked like all his Christmases had come at once. I didn't know if I could do it, but I was sure as hell going to try.

Johnny lay down on the padded bench his cock pointing skyward at the thought of a Hazel sandwich. Leith forced a very reluctant Pablo to lubricate my ass with his tongue and once he got over his initial aversion he really got into it, sometimes even lapping against my cunt lips, I suspect to suck out some of the man spunk that was oozing from them.

Once I was sufficiently wet, I spooned some of the spunk out with my fingers and spread it over my sphincter, pushing my fingers inside. There was no point hesitating and I squatted over Johnny's cock and lowered my ass. It hurt like nothing I'd ever felt before but I knew I had to do it. I gritted my teeth, I thought of Mother England, I swore I'd never do anything like this again, I berated a God that didn't make assholes self-lubricating, and then, with one almighty roar, Johnny was inside. It was only the head and I felt like my ass was on fire but I knew with time and a few deep breaths it would all be good eventually. It was more than good. By the time I had managed to stuff his entire prick in my bowels, I was bobbing up and down really getting into the swing of anal sex. Leith was pleased with my obvious progress but wanted the full show.

Lucky was next. Bobby had slicked up his cock, lubing it with his saliva. Even so, it was going to be an effort fitting it all in my tiny cunt. The men all packed around me, watching as Lucky began to push between my cunt lips, the head disappearing comparatively easily. It was painful but there was the underlying pleasure that was beginning to well up from deep inside me. I knew when I next had an orgasm it would be explosive. I did my breathing exercises as Lucky slowly pushed his way inside my pussy, filling me with more cock than I ever thought possible.

"Shit, you're so tight," he moaned.

Then, he was in. I asked for a short rest to get accustomed to the feeling. I looked over at Leith whose cock was drooling at the sight of his wife being double penetrated.

"You okay, honey?" he asked.

"Better than okay. Come on, Pierre, shove your cock in my mouth, let's get this show on the road."

I have to admit the pain was so excruciating at first I lost track of time. I heard voices whispering, voices shouting, voices groaning. I wanted to step outside my poor battered body and watch me taking three men's cocks. I heard my husband panting and longed to see the look of admiration on his face. Pierre pulled out so I was face to face with my husband being ass fucked like a slut just as I was. Louis was slamming Leith's cunt, pushing us together so our mouths met and he could taste the other men's spunk on my tongue.

"How's it feel to be our slut, boy?" Louis snarled viciously. "Bet you always dreamed of hot cock in that ass of yours, eh, boy? Tell me you want it."

To see a pretty boy using my rugged, handsome man like some cum dump had to be the best ever.

"Take a picture of him," I yelled and I heard the click of a cell phone camera. "Fuck his ass Louis, make him beg for your cock."

Louis was on a high. "I'm gonna breed your ass, man. It's so fuckin' tight. Tell me how you want my cock, man. Tell me."

"I love your cock in my ass, Louis. It's the best feeling ever. Fuck me, mate. Make my ass bleed."

Louis rode him like he was a bucking bronco, pulling his hair until Leith's head snapped back and his mouth opened in pain. Pablo took that as an opportunity to slam his unsatisfied prick down his throat. My man had never sucked a cock all the way down before and he choked, mucous squeezing out the side of his mouth, making spidery patterns whenever Pablo pulled his cock all the way out.

The image was seared into my memory as Pierre blocked the view, pushing his cock back into my mouth. I just hoped Leith was in as much pain/pleasure as I was. Pierre was the first to shoot his cock snot deep into my throat allowing me to watch my husband again, still in the throes of having his ass reamed by a sweating Louis, also now sucking Bobby's cock while Pablo smacked his ass.

"Breed the fucker," I shouted. "Make him your cock whore."

The cacophony of curses, groans and swearing was reaching a pitch. I was going to come. I couldn't help it, I shouted to God and all the angels as my cunt muscles clamped down on Lucky's prick and my sphincter did much the same around Johnny. They both flooded my insides with their warm slime within seconds of each other. I never wanted it to end. I looked across at Leith whose face was dripping with Bobby's sperm as Louis shuddered his spunk up his ass. Leith's twisted smile said everything I needed to know.

"Happy birthday, lover. I hope you got what you wanted," I said.

"And more," he replied.

"I hope you'll come and visit us some time in Paris," Louis said as he pulled out of Leith's ass.

"And please think of Paradise Palms as your second home," Bobby added.

They all broke into 'Happy Birthday, Leith' to which he smiled shyly.

I wasn't concentrating on the words because I was already thinking ahead to the adventures we would have with Matt the taxi driver on the trip back, wondering whether he'd like to watch my husband and Con from the sex shop breeding each other's ass. I knew I would.

The Groom Always Comes Twice

"I fucked the ass off her. Redhead, tits like…" I drew a picture in the air with my hands. "She was fuckin' insatiable, man. I thought I'd rub the skin off my dick. Stayed all weekend."

"You gonna see her again?" one of the young office juniors asked.

"Nah, I don't do anyone twice."

"Can I have her phone number, Justin?" one of the computer geeks asked.

"What d'ya think I am, a pimp for the IT department?"

It was a running joke. Every week one of the guys from IT would ask for the phone number of that weekend's fuckfest, and I'd turn him down with the same response. Just as the Monday morning sex debrief was a ritual to our firm. It began with us execs boasting about our cocksmanship until one by one they'd all married except for me and Milton. We were the youngest and the best looking. We both had an uneasy relationship as the cock of the walk although Milton was much less expansive about his conquests than I was. In fact, he didn't get laid every week. I did. He didn't go into graphic descriptions of whether they took it up the ass and whether they swallowed. I did.

In fact, he was so reticent about his sex life the rumor raced through the company that he was gay. The one thing Ron Bax ~~& Son~~ did not appreciate, was a gay employee. That was why the '& Son' in the firm's name had been crossed through or erased as far as possible. Ron's pride and joy and the man to carry on the family name and the family company had come out at the ripe old age of twenty, telling his dad that it was highly unlikely that he could expect any grandchildren unless he and his boyfriend decided on surrogacy.

Dad went apoplectic with rage; the son was disinherited and thrown out of the house, his name removed from the company letterhead and all visible signs including those on the sides of the company's trucks. Problem was that Ron is a cheap bastard sometimes and the huge sign on the front of the building made from inlaid gloss ceramic tiles from the Mediterranean had a heritage order against it so it could not be changed. It had become a local landmark and featured in many a travel guide. It was one of the few remaining works by the Art Deco master Giuseppe Strambio, and one of the best in the country.

Without permission, Ron had a painter draw a thick black line through the '& Son' to show the world he had disowned his only boy. There were threats of prosecution, demands the paint be removed, all sorts of bribes going back and forth until Ron cried 'enough' and said that he would 'blow the bastard sky high' unless he was allowed to keep his very public rejection of his son. Everyone knew he was serious and decided they could live with the desecration rather than live with no Strambio at all. In time, it became an even greater talking point.

Of more importance to the folk who were employed at Ron Bax ~~& Son~~, it did not pay to show the slightest same-gender proclivities. There had been a witch hunt at the firm and anyone with the slightest effeminacy was dismissed although reasons given were of a more serious nature. Most people didn't complain because they received a rather substantial payout so they wouldn't charge unfair dismissal, their reference was glowing and they were usually glad to escape the terrible homophobic atmosphere.

Thus began the Monday morning sex talkfest. All the men who wanted to keep their lucrative employment began to boast about the previous weekend's sexual escapades, each more outrageous than the other. It eventually evolved into oral erotica with the cubicles in the men's toilets echoing to the pants and groans of executives and mail boys relieving their frustration and their envy. If someone had drilled glory holes in the cubicle walls, they would probably have drowned in the collected spooge. I even recommended to my best female friend in the world, Kylie, that she set herself up in one of the cubicles and relieve the men for a price, but she's an old-fashioned girl and would have done it for free.

See, one of the reasons Kylie and I get on so well together is because we're both sluts – for cock. But you would have guessed that already. That's why I had to lie about my sexual adventures. Mind you, the lies were minor. Like, the partners I had on the weekend had no cunts because they were male. But I embellished by giving them vaginas that I sucked, licked and otherwise fucked, whereas it was cock I licked and sucked and ass that I fucked. Along with the usual things you do with a human mouth. Okay, maybe a few unusual things as well.

Over the years I'd built up quite a reputation as a ladies' man although some of the others must have questioned the authenticity of my stories, even if only in their minds. Sometimes I would bring a pair of pussy juice soaked panties for show and tell, courtesy of Kylie. They were usually passed around to the groans and sniffs of the growing band of married men, and they usually disappeared at some stage into someone's coat pocket. I didn't mind, I had no use for them apart from a prop for my dissembling.

It's not that I can't get women, in fact, I'm considered prime beef by the female of the species but I'm just not made that way. It's nothing personal as I told Kylie on the couple of occasions she's tried it on with me. It's genetics. It's men that get the blood pumping to my dick: masculine good looks, stubble, plump round asses, hard pecs, muscular biceps, and best of all, hard pulsing cocks that squirt my favorite liquid – thick hot spunk.

Fortunately for me, I attract as many men as I do women. Rarely do I turn them down. I'm not indiscriminate, they have to be breathing, but if you ask then you're unlikely to be refused. My date book is full until well into next year although if it's just a quickie in an adult bookshop or an alley or just about anywhere public or private, then try me. You'll find I'm very amenable. Oh, you want to bring a friend. Sure, why not?

Kylie is my female equivalent. If I had been twins, she would be my sister. She's as hot as I am, and just as promiscuous.

I think it's my good looks and fit body, plus the lascivious stares from female co-workers that convince most of my male colleagues that there's not much exaggeration in my sex tales. Only Niles Carson has any doubts which he voices vociferously to anyone who'll listen. Niles is the thorn in my side on two counts. The second is the one just listed coupled with the fact he's always trying to expose me. The main reason is that he's hotter than hell in a heat wave. He's just so me that every time I see him my cock wants to shoot in my trousers.

He was one of the first to marry. Impossibly beautiful wife. The kid came six months later so there was a lot of nudge nudge wink wink, but with Niles' dedication to the company and the hours he kept, his wife felt a little neglected. This was the story on the gossip grapevine at any rate, and she found herself a more stay-at-home hubby and a quickie divorce was organized. Niles never seemed particularly heartbroken by the split-up. God, how I wanted to be his wife or his husband or even his foot stool.

Avoid him, you think? Impossible. I'm Laurel to his Hardy, Abbott to his Costello, Gaga to his Lady. You get what I mean? We are so good together the company, in their infinite wisdom, put us in offices side by side and gave us interlocking jobs. We're the go-to guys when something needs fixing.

If I'm that indispensable, you'd think my job would be safe. No, afraid not. I only got the position because my predecessor was one of those unceremoniously dumped when the Gay Free Zone edict came into being. This company has the potential to be bigger than Jesus, meaning Steve Jobs not the other guy, and I want to be part of it.

You can see my problem.

The real shit-hit-the fan start to my troubles began the day that fellow bachelor, Milton Locke, clapped me on the back and said, "I've finally done it, Justin." I had no idea what he was talking about. "I've asked Maureen to marry me. She said 'yes.' I want you to be my Best Man."

I was shocked on so many levels, not the least of which is that everyone thought Milton was a closet case. His marriage would leave me the sole bachelor in upper management and rapidly approaching the age at which I would be expected to settle down, my wild oats having been well and truly sown.

Dredging up as much enthusiasm as I could muster, I beamed at his news, albeit on low beam. "Congratulations, that's wonderful news." I sent my mind swirling through my memory banks to conjure up an image of said Maureen but came up blank. "You and Maureen will be very happy."

"So, will you?"

"Will I what?"

"Be my Best Man?"

I'd never been particularly close to Milton so I didn't know why he was asking. Sure, I always shot the breeze with him if we were ever in the same room together and occasionally helped him out with a problem, but I never went out of my way…

He must have seen the puzzled look on my face. "I don't have many friends in the city and you've always been—"

He didn't finish the sentence because I interrupted before it became a total embarrassment to both of us. "I'd be honored."

Milton seemed just as grateful for my intervention.

"Let's do lunch and we can iron out the details."

It all seemed straightforward enough. I'd turn up at the wedding, stand next to Milton, hand him the rings, say a few slightly raunchy things at the reception, dance with his new wife, maybe squeeze her butt and tell her that it's just as well I didn't meet her first, and then wave the happy couple off on their honeymoon.

"You haven't thought this through at all, have you?" Kylie said when I met her after work at our favorite watering hole, where the clientele was young enough that whichever gender hit on them, they took it as a compliment. A polite "No thanks" was all that was necessary if you weren't interested. No one took offence.

"What do you mean?" I asked.

Kylie and I almost never looked at one another while we spoke in this bar, our eyes too busy searching out prospective partners, but she turned to me when she replied, "You'll be expected to organize the bachelor party."

"So?"

"At the very least you'll have to suck some tit in front of your buddies from work, maybe indulge in a bit of a titty fuck. At the worst it will mean a blow job or a fuck.

Unless you want to look like the big fag you are to your boss."

I felt the blood drain from my face. "What am I going to do?"

"My suggestion would be to go along with the whole charade but develop Dengue Fever the night before the bachelor party."

"You find this amusing, don't you?"

"Highly," she said.

Milton had never struck me as the particularly promiscuous type; he always kept his own counsel on Monday mornings. Perhaps he wouldn't want a stripper, or he'd be content with just a visit to a pole dance club where he could ogle the girls, stick a few bucks in their G-strings and leave as chaste as he entered.

Kylie shot my theory down in flames. "In your dreams, honey."

Those dreams were about to become nightmares. Milton had not only invited Ron Bax himself, but also a good half dozen of his closest colleagues at the firm, including Niles Carson.

"I thought the cunt was a faggot," Bax said to me in his office the next day. "If I could have found any proof, his sorry ass would have been out the door. I hear you're organizing the bachelor party. Better make it something sizzling; me and the boys are pretty eager to watch you in action to pick up a few hints." He was crass enough to wink.

I had to tread carefully. "Listen, about that. I'm not sure Milton is a stripper sort of guy."

"Who gives a fuck?" Bax snapped. "If I go to a party I want titty, I want cunt. I want to get my knob polished. If Milton doesn't like it, he can leave."

"It is his party," I tried weakly.

"Not when I'm paying for it. I want a classy broad who'll go the whole way. None of this vibrator show shit, or the titty fuck. I want a woman who'll bend over and take us all. You get me a woman like that and I'll pay what she asks."

Shit, this was worse than I thought. Dengue Fever was looking like a real option, especially when Niles bailed me up in the lunch room when I was getting a coffee. "I hear the bachelor party is going to be something else," he smirked. "I'll be able to watch you in action and see where my marriage went wrong."

"If you're going to be watching me, Niles, then that's where your problem was right from the start."

He almost choked on his coffee because I'd as good as called him a fag.

"I'm on to you, Justin," he seethed. "You don't fool me."

He stormed out of the room. I knew I'd have to watch my back.

Over the next few weeks I became more and morose as I could see no way out of my dilemma. I couldn't fake a serious illness in either my family or myself as Niles would be sure to check. I could always kill him but I didn't fancy playing bitch boy to some tattooed punk in prison for the rest of my life. There was always a groin injury, and on a number of occasions I was horrified to discover I had my dinner knife raised ready to strike between my legs.

I didn't allow my concern to affect my sex life to any great extent although I did manage to bore a few partners with my distraction. My explanation usually met with a sneer about 'closet cases.' I deserved that. In fact, I did think about coming out to everyone at work just for the relief from the stress, maybe go out with a bang by sucking off all the guys after one of my raunchy recollections on a Monday morning. Then I looked at my expensive apartment and my credit card bills and knew that was not an option.

Niles didn't help with his "I'm hoping the stripper's a beauty because I can hardly wait to sink my cock inside her," after which he'd grab a handful of his crotch and I'd suddenly feel as if all the oxygen had been sucked out of the air.

Then I had one of those ideas that change the history of the world, like Darwin and the evolution of the species or Newton and the idea of gravity. Mine was simplicity itself and I could hardly wait to tell Kylie.

I have to say she took it well. "You want me to what?" Her shock went on for a whole paragraph of question marks. When I didn't respond because I knew perfectly well her question was rhetorical, she said, "What do you think I am? A whore?"

"No, you're a slut," I responded kindly, "So why not make some money out of it for a change."

"How much are we talking here?" She was a mercenary bitch.

Bax had given me a figure but I under-quoted to give me some wriggle room to haggle if necessary. Kylie was always broke so I knew that a cash incentive would attract her attention.

I wrote the figure on a beer mat, shoving it toward her. "You're shittin' me?" I shook my head. The next words she uttered let me know she was thinking it over. "Whose army do I have to fuck for that kind of money?"

"Just a few guys."

"How many constitutes a few, Justin?"

"Less than you took on at last year's rave party."

"Remind me how many that was again."

It was a dozen over a twelve-hour period. She wouldn't have the luxury of that time span at the bachelor party.

"So how many exactly?" she persisted.

"Seven or eight."

"Pretty small bachelor party."

"Milton doesn't have many friends."

"That's a blessing, at least." Then her suspicious nature got the better of her. "They all dogs?"

"The opposite, in fact. One of the guys…" I told her about Niles and that certainly perked her interest. Good looking was always a bonus.

"What's your cut of the door?"

"I don't want any of it," I said. "It's not about the money. It's about saving my job."

"How does me playing stripper sex goddess to your workmates save your job?"

"You fake having wild abandoned sex with me."

I went on to explain how easy it would be to fake the sex with her head in my lap or else her seated on my groin without any penetration. She snickered as I delicately explained it all. "Wouldn't it just be easier to stick it in?"

"Eww. You're my best friend. Plus you're a woman."

"You got a problem with that?"

"I don't see you out every weekend eating pussy," I replied.

"Okay, I get your point. Let me think about it and I'll get back to you."

I expected she'd make me sweat over her decision for at least a week although I was pretty confident the cash would swing it, so I was surprised when, later that night, Kylie rang to say, "I'll do it for…" quoting a price that was still within Bax's range.

I agreed to her demands but reiterated she'd have to get some sort of costume for at least a pretense of stripping although as long as she gave me a list of music,

I'd organize to have the sound system and CDs set-up for her.

My good mood returned almost immediately and I congratulated myself on getting out of a very tight and very dangerous situation. My change did not go without notice, Niles needling me at every opportunity. "Whatever trick it is you have up your sleeve, I'll expose you. You're a fuckin' fraud, Justin."

His face was in mine and he was frothing at the mouth. I could have just leaned forward and kissed him. Instead I thumbed the spittle from his lips. "There, that's better," I said. "You shouldn't get so angry, Niles, it spoils your handsome features."

I don't know what made me do it but I was more than rewarded by the look of surprise on his face. I walked back to my office more than satisfied that I'd upset his equilibrium for a change. It was petty payback so I wondered why I was so reluctant to wipe his saliva off my thumb. Was it because of the current of attraction I felt? Nah, couldn't be. Niles was as straight as an arrow. It must be me projecting my lust onto him.

Without thinking, I put my thumb in my mouth to suck it and that's where it was when Niles passed my door and glanced in. The shock on both our faces must have been amusing to anyone who'd been watching us. I could have saved the situation by pretending I'd injured my thumb and was sucking the blood off or some other variation but instead I yanked it out of my mouth in such a hurried and guilty fashion it was quite obvious what I was doing.

Once he'd passed, I screwed my face up in disgust that I'd been caught. I was getting careless, giving him ammunition to use against me. If only he wasn't so fuckin' hot. Yeah, I'd had better, but this guy was the full deck. I actually liked socializing with him before he became the arrogant asshole who threatened to unmask me. We had a number of shared interests although the one I most wanted to share, our bodies, was not on his list of future goals. Bastard!

I don't know whether he went out of his way to avoid me over the next few weeks but I ran into him much less frequently and when I did he was less obnoxious, not exactly pleasant, but more as if he couldn't work me out. Whatever it was I was glad of the truce, I didn't want to hate him. Once the bachelor party was out of the way I could relax and we could get a bit of perspective back into our working relationship.

Kylie wouldn't tell me what she planned for her routine and I had to admit I didn't push it. I'd already told Bax I'd found a very classy piece of work who was willing to take on the entire party provided she was treated with respect.

"Respect?" Bax blustered. "She's a fuckin' whore, what will she do with a non-cash commodity like respect?"

I was merely trying to protect Kylie from the more blatant exploitation that I'd heard went on at these sorts of events. "What I meant was, she's doesn't like it rough and doesn't want any marks. Okay?"

"But anything else goes?"

"That's my understanding." I could have added no whips, no bondage and no farm animals but I thought that might give him ideas.

"Good. As long as she sucks my cock, I'm happy."

"That she'll do," I said, to his obvious satisfaction.

In the event, she did much, much more.

I was as nervous as hell in the lead-up to the big night. Milton's prospective bride rang me to ensure there would be no untoward behavior at the party. I assured her it was a tame affair because all the men in attendance, bar me, were married men, and she was placated by that. Not so the wives of the other men who knew better what went on when men farewell a compatriot from bachelorhood.

They believed me when I said it would be raunchy but tame. By being upfront that a stripper was involved they were happy to believe she would merely reveal all, allow the men a feel of her tits and probably give Milton a blow job. They were prepared to allow that much leeway and no more while commiserating about Milton cheating on his bride-to-be, Maureen. I guess they saw themselves as having been in that situation before their own marriages.

I couldn't pick up Kylie and drive her to the hotel because I had to be on hand to welcome the guests, so I'd hired a limo for her knowing that would make her night. The venue was a posh room in one of the city's top hotels. I'd already warned the front desk of our intentions and slipped a substantial tip to the counter staff and the bellboys to treat Kylie with every courtesy.

The only unknown was Kylie herself. In the days leading up to the party I sat her down and reiterated how important this whole façade was to my future and that it had to pass off without a hitch. I couldn't afford to be outed, so her performance when we pretended to have sex had to be convincing. Therefore no excessive drinking, no drugs, and no giggling.

"I'll be totally professional," she said.

Still, I had a sinking feeling in the pit of my stomach.

Then the night arrived and it was too late to do anything but push ahead. Milton had confided that he was up for a bit of fun and games if that was in the offering, pleased when I assured him it was. Everyone was impressed with the hotel room and the endless supply of alcohol. In case I disgraced myself, I took the necessary pills to keep my cock in a rampant state although I sensed that one look at a naked Niles would keep it there for most of the night without the added stimulus. However, you can never take too many precautions. Or too many pills.

The porn movies were fairly vanilla, although the gangbang component must have given the guys some idea what to expect. Bax, of course, lowered the whole tone of the evening by telling everyone he'd paid enough that they could 'fuck the bitch to death' if they wanted. I spent far too much time undoing the damage.

The group had begun drinking and carousing around 7pm, I made sure there was enough substantial finger food to soak up some of the alcohol, so by the time Kylie was due to arrive around 8.30pm the party had become quite rowdy, Bax repeating he'd paid for the stripper at least twenty times while the married men encouraged one another in their foolish bravado about how they were going to 'do the bitch over.' There were five of them plus Bax and myself. Niles remained remarkably quiet not joining in the raucous behavior although every time I looked over to where he sat patiently nursing his drink, he was looking my way.

I admit I was nervous. Even though I'd had a bit to drink myself to dull the pain, I still jumped when the phone in the room rang, the signal that Kylie was on her way to the suite. I went out to meet her at the elevator, knocked out by how classy she looked. She was all in red, from the long dress that almost reached the ground, though her red high heels, to the lipstick. Her hair was piled high on her head.

I didn't say it but I did think she looked a little too cultured for our party crowd. She read my mind anyway.

"Don't worry, Jus. The real outfit is underneath. I thought if I turned up looking like a lady they may be less inclined to act like trash."

"Good luck with that, Bax has been encouraging them. He's an old-world sexist so he's the one to be careful of. Oh, and you'll know Niles the moment you enter the room."

"He's the cute one you fancy, right?"

"Blue balls," I admitted.

Kylie was correct, her outfit did have an amazing calming effect on the group, even on Bax who kissed her gloved hand like a true gentlemen. I think the others were a little intimidated by her class and her beauty. Niles raised an eyebrow in my direction as if to imply he was impressed with my taste in strippers. Still, I didn't trust him.

That Kylie was a hit was apparent, especially when Milton sidled up to me to whisper, "You think it's too late to cancel the wedding and marry her?" He pumped my hand. "Thank you so much. This is going to be the best night of my life." That didn't auger well for his marriage.

After she'd mingled just enough to get the boys onside, she downed another drink. I say another because earlier, when she stepped out of the elevator, I smelled liquor on her breath. I showed her to the bedroom so she could change, hugging her good luck, feeling the slight tremble beneath her calm exterior. "You'll be great

Kyles," I encouraged. "Maybe open up great new career opportunities. Stock Exchange by day, bachelor parties by night."

"That Niles guy is totally to die for," she smiled nervously.

"Don't think I'm not jealous as hell," I said.

"I'll knock on the bedroom door when I'm ready. Start the music then."

I'd burned her chosen tracks onto a CD so there would be no longueurs in the routine. Nothing worse than a stripper forced to wave her booty to silence while a DJ changes the music. Back in the main room, I lowered the lights, switching some off altogether, increasing the mood of expectation. Voices were muted now and the men had arranged themselves on the lounge suite and in chairs around an area I'd mapped out for the performance. Milton, looking terrified but anticipatory, had pride of place on his own in a padded chair at the edge of the play area.

Kylie's knocks meant my future was secure or fucked. I took a deep breath and turned on the music, adjusting the volume as it poured out through the speakers. I expected Kylie to burst out the door but instead it opened slowly and she popped through the door as if she was just coming home. There was a collective gasp because the sophisticated woman now looked like a college girl from the 1950s, right down to her ponytail and her packed sweater.

Unfortunately for me, it made her even less erotic in my eyes. I was grateful now I'd taken the medicinal aphrodisiac. It didn't matter what I thought because it was obviously having an effect on her targeted audience. I have to admit it was all a bit of a blur, I was so apprehensive I was wound up like a spring toy ready to pop.

It seemed no time at all that Kylie had her sweater off, her bra unhooked courtesy of Ron Bax, and her tits in Milton's face before she was giving every man in the room a go at her knockers. My work colleagues kneaded them, squeezed the nipples, sucked them, rubbed their faces in them, while yahooing like people who'd never seen tits before. I had to admit, they were an impressive sight although I'd seen them countless times before. Kylie and I had often attended the sorts of parties together where it was not uncommon for the guests to remove their clothing before the end of the evening.

There was an air of expectation as she completed her circuit of the room except for me. She straddled my hips, grinding her pelvis against my unenthusiastic crotch, while pushing her tits in my face. I massaged them slowly, noticing her nipples were as erect as I'd ever seen them, before leaning in to suck them like the others but with a little more finesse, teasing rather than going at them like a bull at a gate. I saw Niles watching with interest out of the corner of my eye.

Kylie gave a little moan as I bit down on the nipples which led to a round of applause. Kylie pulled away but not before pulling my face into her cleavage to much ribald laughter.

I can do this. I can do this.

It became my mantra.

By the time she was down to her panties, which even I could see were already soaked with her juices, she was so turned on by the manhandling I was beginning to think of myself as a heterosexual for the night. Then she took her panties off and my house of cards came crashing down. Sure I'd seen her pussy before but not when I had known I was going to be up close and personal.

She put her foot on the arm of the chair in which Ron Bax sat like cock of the walk, displaying her bald pussy for his delectation. He petted her mound before pushing aside her flaps to get his thumb on her clit. Kylie moaned her appreciation and I thought she was about to come but pulled away at the last moment to display herself to Milton. He reached out as if afraid the naked woman in front of him would disappear at any moment. He couldn't believe his luck if the look on his face was anything to go by as he buried his fingers in her pussy, frigging her until he held his slimy fingers aloft in triumph. He put them in his mouth sucking them contentedly, his trousers tenting.

Kylie gave every man an opportunity to play with her moist cunt, Niles making an ostentatious show of sniffing and sucking his fingers, daring me to better him. As Kylie displayed her cunt to me I could smell how ripe she was for fucking. She winked in encouragement. It was only two fingers after all. I pushed between her wet warm folds, sinking into her cunt. I felt disloyal but I imagined I was finger fucking Niles's asshole all the while I sawed in and out of Kylie's cunt. It was the closest I'd ever been to a woman.

There was a catch in Kylie's breath before she began to tremble, her groans becoming louder until she panted, "Yes, yes, yes. Do it. Fuck my pussy. Oh, baby. Your fingers feel so good. Bring me off, honey. Yeah, just like that. Good, good."

She wailed and I felt her pussy tighten around my fingers. Her body trembled for a good twenty seconds before she managed to disengage from my hand. I was lucky that the group whistled and stamped their feet in appreciation of my expertise in bringing her to orgasm, that no one noticed me wipe my fingers on the edge of the lounge chair and that I didn't put them in my mouth. No one except Niles.

Once she'd recovered, Kylie danced over to the wedding boy, kneeling in front of him as she unzipped his fly to pull down his trousers. There was a spot of damp on his briefs where his cock had leaked. Kylie leaned in and licked it, running her lips along the outline of his hard cock, before clenching the elastic waist band in her teeth and dragging it down so his cock sprang free.

For such a timid guy, Milton had really lucked out in the size department. He wasn't as big as me but he was thicker.

Kylie was impressed because she couldn't wait to get him out of his trousers and briefs. "Take your shirt off, honey, I love to see a man's chest while I suck his cock."

Milton was totally naked in a matter of seconds, dumping his clothes on the floor beside his chair in his haste to get the 'night of his life.' I knew Kylie was showing off as she licked his shaft and played with his balls bringing the poor guy to the boil before backing off. She licked the head, sticky with his oozing pre-cum, before taking him deep in her throat. Milton bucked as his cock stretched her mouth wide and his cock disappeared between her lips. He pressed his hands on her head obviously wanting to keep her there but also attempting to pry her loose because he didn't want it to be over too soon.

Kylie took pity on him and released his cock, running her tongue across his nipples, biting them so he gave little yelps of pain, spoiling him for whatever sex life he was destined to have with his new wife. When she thought his balls had calmed down sufficiently, she kneeled on all fours, displaying her vulnerable cunt to the room as she took Milton in her mouth again.

It was all the invitation Bax required. "Boss's prerogative," he said as he quickly stripped out of his clothes, his tubby body as uninviting as his stubby little prick. Kneeling behind her, he smeared his cockhead with her leaking juices, then rammed his prick into her. It was fascinating to watch my boss acting like an animal with my best friend but it certainly wasn't a turn on, although the other men in the room were in various stages of undress, jerking their cocks as they awaited a turn.

I realized I was the only man still fully clothed, glancing over to Niles who was totally naked, smug in the superiority of his looks and muscular body. His cock was a beauty and finally my cock began to stretch in interest. It had lain dormant for too long. It would be embarrassing to strip only to reveal my cock was limp.

I kept staring at Niles as he milked his prodigious weapon until my cock reached its full potential and then I removed my trousers. The look on Niles's face as he saw my hard prick was priceless. For a moment, I thought I saw his mouth water but I was hallucinating. Lack of blood to my brain because it was all in my cock thanks to Niles.

I stroked myself slowly, pretending it was his hand, trying not to watch my best friend on the receiving end of my bastard boss's dick. Milton screamed he was coming and Kylie pushed her face into his pubes until I saw the muscles in her throat taking his load. Milton thrashed about in awe, mumbling, "She's swallowed my spunk. She swallowed it."

Like a dance where guys tap each other on the shoulder to get a turn with the most popular girl, one of the other men tapped Milton to move, taking his place on the chair, Bax appeared in no hurry to give up her pussy.

And so the sexual musical chairs continued, Kylie blowing guys and taking others in her cunt until she was starting to leak spunk from both ends. I watched enviously as Niles lay her on her back and fucked her like an expert making her moan for real, leaning in to kiss her, nibble her ear and whisper who knew what. Whatever it was she whispered back, sharing something she'd never shared with me. Maybe they'd become an item.

And then it was my turn. Kylie crawled over to where I sat. I was so afraid my dick would shrink but with Kylie's head in my lap, the Viagra did its job. She pushed my cock down between my legs while she made a tunnel with her hand as if it was wrapped around my prick stroking it up and down, her lips supposedly around the head and the first few inches. It was a masterly performance from Kylie who even gave the appearance of choking at one stage when I thrust a little too hard. I hoped my performance of orgasm was as convincing as hers. I didn't want to appear to come too quickly but neither did I want to stretch it out for so long I may get caught out.

We both played our parts to perfection, me thrashing about and grunting between clenched teeth while she pretended to gag. Secretly she pulled my cock out from between my legs, spitting on the knob to give it a slimed look. As she bobbed her head up, she ran the back of her hand across her mouth as if to wipe away the residue. I looked up to see Niles in the background smiling smugly giving my performance silent applause.

Bastard.

I suppose I was a bit too eager when I announced, "If everyone's had a turn, I suppose we should thank the amazing Kylie…"

"Shit, no," Bax said. "The party's just beginning. I could go again. Right guys?"

I should have known it was all too easy.

"I think you need to ask Kylie because I know she has another show tonight and we don't want to wear her out."

I hoped she'd take the hint.

Instead, she said. "Oh, didn't I tell you? They canceled. I'm just getting warmed up, so give me a chance to clean up and we can party all night. What do you say, guys?"

They, of course, were all for it, so my agony was prolonged.

I followed her into the bedroom where she prepared to take a shower. "What are you doing?" I snapped.

"I did what you asked, now I'm going to have some fun."

"But they'll expect me to…"

"What?"

"You know."

"Well, if you fuck as well as you finger there shouldn't be a problem."

"You didn't fake it?"

"No. You've got magic fingers, Jus. Besides, that Niles guy is fucking amazing."

I tried to lighten the mood. "If you marry him, our friendship is over."

She laughed. "Don't think I'm not tempted. Wouldn't work out though. I'm too much of a slut for him. He's looking for a relationship."

"Is that what you two were whispering about?"

"You noticed?"

"Of course, I noticed. I couldn't tear my eyes away from his cock. Tell me, was it as delicious as it looked?"

"Better."

I groaned.

"Now go outside while I shower, get them all in a party mood."

I was bailed up by Niles the moment I went back to the party. The men had slipped their underwear back on in a surprising show of modesty. "Where did you find her? She your girlfriend?"

"Please," I said. "Like I'd let a girlfriend of mine loose with these pigs."

He shrugged. "So? Where'd you find her?"

"She came highly recommended."

"Much classier than the sort of stripper you normally get at a party like this."

"Go to a lot of them do you?"

"Not as many as you, obviously."

"I'm not into public sex," I said with an arrogant air of superiority that I didn't mean.

"You just like to talk about it."

"I want to keep my job."

I walked away from him to get myself a stiff drink, uncomfortably aware of how Niles affected me when he stood too close, like he had been just then. I slipped on my boxers which, for the most part, hid my problem. The guys crowded around me, eager to congratulate me on finding such an accommodating stripper. Bax, in particular, was ecstatic, Milton not far behind, scaring me that he might actually call off the wedding in the forlorn hope he could pursue Kylie.

"She's incredible," he whispered. "I'll never forget her. Thanks for the experience, Justin. She's way out of my league but it's good just once in a lifetime to have that experience."

Shit! I'd accidentally done a good deed.

I didn't have time to wallow in my saint-like behavior because a refreshed Kylie slithered her way back into contention. She hadn't bothered to dress, she was hot for cock and these guys were just the men to give it to her. I'd never watched her, really watched her, before. Sure, we'd done the party thing together but I was much too engrossed in my own pleasure to watch what my best female friend was up to. It was erotic watching her wrap her lips around hard cock, even more so watching guys bury themselves up to their balls in her wet pussy, especially when Kylie verbalized her pleasure. It was particularly arousing for me to watch Niles banging her cunt again, whispering sweet nothings in her ear until she was giggling.

I nursed my drink seated in Milton's VIP chair, stroking my naked cock as I watched Niles' balls bang against Kylie's cunt flaps, wondering what his cock would feel like buried in my ass. When he pulled out I noticed the string of cum from her pussy lips to the knob of his cock. What I wanted most in the world was to get down and lick it off. What I wanted least was to hear Bax say, "Come on, Justin, don't be a party pooper, you haven't fucked the bitch yet. Show us your routine."

I must have looked shocked because Kylie immediately covered for me.

"He wanted you guys to have all the fun first. He's going to drive me home, he'll get special service then."

"Bullshit," Bax said. "Your cunt will be so sloppy, it won't be worth fucking."

Always the charmer, my boss.

I thought Kylie would put up more of a fight, but she must have sensed he wouldn't take no for an answer. "Okay, you're the boss," she said advancing on me.

She managed to seat herself in my lap, my cock pushed down under her ass, rubbing her cunt around my groin to make it appear I was embedded inside her. She didn't dare bob up and down because it would be apparent I was not fucking her so I thrust as if I wanted to do all the work as she ground her body down on my groin.

It was convincing enough, particularly with Kylie mouthing how much she liked my big long cock in her cunt. Until, that is, Niles stopped the show with, "Hold on a second, Justin. Here, let me help you." He kneeled in front of us, plunging his hand between my legs, gripping my cock so that I felt a spark of electricity in my balls just from his touch, held it aloft just beneath Kylie's pulsing cunt lips, and said, "It must have fallen out. Here, Kylie, just squat down and it'll be right up inside your cunt again." He squeezed my cock as if to say he wasn't fooled by my little act. He was keeping me hard as steel in preparation for Kylie and within seconds I was buried inside my first ever cunt.

Kylie was breathing hard. "Oh, fuck, that is so good." She moved slowly up and down, milking me with her pussy muscles. I threw my head back, unable to do anything except attempt to get my head around the fact I was fucking my very best female friend, my first cunt, and I was actually getting off on it. Okay, it wasn't a man's asshole, and it wasn't my choice but if I had to do it, then I'd enjoy it just as Kylie seemed to be.

I started fucking her hard, like I would any guy who was on the end of my prick. "Take it bitch," I muttered. "I know you want my cock bad. Feel it, bitch. You like that? Want it harder?"

She nodded, biting her lips to stave off her orgasm.

Her cunt was sloppy from all the guys who'd dumped inside her tonight and I was having trouble with traction. The way it was going I wouldn't come for ages. That was obviously fine with Kylie who seemed to be in a world of her own brought about, I suspected, from finally getting me to fuck her. She was screaming now in genuine delight. Even if I wasn't the best fuck she'd ever had, I was the most unexpected. The other men watched in amazement as she screamed her orgasm, begging me to keep fucking her until she came again and again. She must have known this was a once only opportunity and wanted to make the most of it. That was fine by me because I could tell from the looks on the other guys' faces, they thought I had some magic moves with my cock. Only Niles stood apart from the adoring masses.

Okay, so I'd never get Niles but…

"Hey, Niles," I summoned. "Get your scrawny ass over here, buddy. The bitch is on fire. Too much for one man to handle, even one as good as me. Grab that lotion on the table, oil her butthole and join me fucking her into oblivion."

Kylie tensed, mouthing 'You bastard' but I knew she'd been double penetrated before – and loved it. I sat still, my cock still hard as Niles rubbed his fingers into her asshole, loosening her up for his cock. He slathered his shaft until it was slimy enough to slide into her tight hole. I felt his cock rub against mine through the membrane between her anal canal and her cunt. I nearly shot my load just feeling that close to his magnificent prick.

"Oh, man, she's so fuckin' tight," he moaned.

I remained still as Niles slid all the way inside her ass until his balls were knocking against mine. Kylie nodded when the pain subsided enough that we could continue. I began a gentle fucking motion but Niles had to do most of the work. I knew the friction of his cock against mine, even second hand, would get me off. He looked me in the eye as he fucked in and out, almost as if he was imagining it was my ass he was penetrating. Kylie must have realized something was up because she saw I wasn't looking at her but over her shoulder.

She leaned in to whisper in my ear. "He fancies you, you know."

"What?" I mouthed.

"He wants to fuck you."

Kylie arched her back so I could see Niles again. He nodded his head as if to acknowledge what Kylie had just said.

Suddenly, I just wanted this over. I thumbed Kylie's clit as I sawed my cock in and out of her, Niles picking up speed, Kylie's body throbbing between us. We were all panting until Kylie threw her head back and juddered in the most intense orgasm of the night. Her spasms finally brought me to the edge and I shot my load deep into the spunky recesses of her cunt while Niles blew up her rear.

That pretty much sealed Kylie's cunt for the night. She hobbled off to the bathroom while the guys dressed. Some had already returned to the suburbs and their wives, Milton and Bax wanting one last go at her. They joined her in the shower from where sounds of much sexual activity emanated.

"Ask if I can have her phone number, man," One of the guys said, clapping me on the back as he headed out the door for home leaving me and Niles alone together.

"You bastard," I said.

"Hey, if I had to fuck her, so did you."

"It didn't look like it was exactly a chore for you. You went back for seconds and thirds."

"It wasn't unpleasant. Besides, I needed to lay Bax's suspicions to rest."

"He thinks you're gay?" I asked.

"He caught me coming out of a gay bar a few weeks back."

"What, you're bi?"

"Nah, totally gay," Niles admitted.

"That's why you've been an absolute cunt to me for the past few weeks?"

"I'm so sick of playing Bax's games."

"Tonight?"

"My first time. I stayed hard imagining I was fucking you."

I laughed out loud. "Me, too. What about your wife?"

"Just a friend. She wanted her baby to be born legit. I did it as a favor."

"Come here."

I grabbed Niles, mashing my mouth against his, desperate to taste the man I'd craved for so long, the man who'd given me so many nightmares as well as so many wet dreams. It was a kiss like no other and I never wanted it to end. I ran my hands down his naked back to his butt, squeezing his rock solid cheeks, wanting to bury my tongue and my cock between those beautiful mounds. He had much the same idea and I opened my legs wider as his finger stroked my butthole.

"The room's booked for the night, what's say we call up room service and put it on Bax's tab? Get to know each other a little better once those three in the bathroom have gone?" I suggested.

"I'd like to get to know you a whole lot better, Justin," he said, cupping my balls.

We spent half an hour trying to keep our hands off each other as we cleaned up the mess of leftover food and alcohol, bagging it rather than allowing it to stink the place out overnight. Three rather sheepish partygoers came out of the bedroom, flustered from more than the heat of the shower.

Kylie looked chastened and it was then it struck me that she had betrayed me, she had whispered to Niles to make sure that my cock was inside her instead of faking it, knowing I could do nothing about it.

"Forgive me?" she asked.

I nodded, although I wasn't sure I did. She'd played her part for me, then tricked me into giving her what she'd craved for years. Our relationship would certainly have a new dynamic. I wasn't sure as yet what that dynamic would be. I told her I'd call her the next day.

Milton pumped my hand in profuse thanks for organizing the bachelor party although Bax had to interrupt to remind him that he'd paid for it all. They left together, headed to their happy heterosexual lives in the suburbs.

I closed the door, leaning against it, glad we were finally alone. Niles pulled me to his solid, muscular chest, reaching behind me to grab the plastic tag. Without letting me go he opened the door to hang the sign in the hallway.

DO NOT DISTURB.

No More Keeping Mum

"What can I say, son? Your mother's a cunt, not to put too fine a point on it, and I know that's not a part of the human anatomy in which you have any interest."

I laughed politely because I'd never come out to my family although it must have been quite obvious to anyone with half a brain – with no brain at all – that I was gay. In fact, I'm a screaming queen, with my 'Oh, Mary' this and 'Get her' that, plus wrists that flap like the wings on a demented seagull. I wasn't fooling anyone, least of all my mother around whom I butched it up as much as I could, taking me well out of my comfort zone. If I ever dropped a spangle in her company, then dad would always cover for me, telling her quietly, "Slight effeminacy, dear, doesn't mean he isn't interested in girls."

Slight effeminacy? Hell, not only had I bought the whole package, I purchased the entire store. Of course, none of this would have been a problem except for my mum. She was, as my dad put it so succinctly, a vagina. She was also one of the richest women on the West Coast and her largesse included a substantial allowance with which I was able to avail myself of the lifestyle of the rich and famous. Fortunately, I lived on the East Coast, allowing my lifestyle to pass unnoticed although my escapades occasionally made the social pages, the only reading matter that interested my mother. I was discreet enough in public that my worst excesses were usually camouflaged and out of sight. I had enough fag hag friends photographed dripping off my arm to fool most people. Or I did until I fell in love.

Gavin is kind, loving, affectionate, caring, considerate; all the synonyms you can come up with, and loves me more than life itself. He also has the biggest cock I've ever seen and fucks me with it like a human tornado. He is handsome as sin, built like a Renaissance sculpture, his butt cheeks a work of art in themselves. His mouth is built for sucking cock – mine – and his verbal dexterity leaves your common porn star sounding tongue tied. I guess I should have been more careful when out on the town with Gavin. In our happiness we failed to take even the most basic precautions: we forgot to take a woman each as a beard.

So the paparazzi plastered shots of me and Gavin with scarcely concealed hints at our relationship status across the social pages of all the major glossy magazines.

Our belated attempt to turn our cozy duo into a cozier quartet via the insertion of two high-profile television actresses was too little and much too late. My mother was not about to be fobbed off with the excuse Gavin was my PA/bodyguard and general dogsbody. "One does not, at least in my experience," she said icily down the phone, "go about sticking one's tongue in the mouth of one's personal assistant whether one is drunk or not. Hired help need to know their place in the overall scheme of things and that is not on the end of their employer's tongue. Especially if one's assistant is of the same gender." Her voice had reached fever pitch by the time she had completed her spiel. There was nothing I could say to appease her, so I kept mum.

I know what you're thinking. I could have told her to take her fortune and shove it into that anatomical cavity in which I had no interest, but then how would I survive? My only skills, and it must be said they are the envy of many a hostess, consist of charm, wit, good looks, and the uncanny ability to throw the best parties since the last Oscars bash. In fact, I organized a few of those for the larger fashion and perfumery companies to enhance their reputations. You see, I know anyone who is worth knowing. I even know a few people who are not worth knowing, but that's another story and belongs in my more drunken and drug-fucked past.

My attempts to outfox my mother brought out the devious in me. Not long after the admonishing phone call from across the country, a young woman gained notoriety by claiming that I was the father of her two-year-old child, conceived during a glitzy drunken opening night party for some musical or the other at which she had been a cocktail waitress. It was a rare miscalculation on my part. The press reaction was screams of laughter at the very notion of me fathering a child even via artificial insemination and although I thought the performance by the actress I paid was worthy of a Meryl Streep, the subterfuge was brought undone by the simple expedient of a scandal sheet comparing my DNA with that of my purported son. The press had stooped to stealing a wine glass I'd used in a restaurant and yanking a number of tufts of hair from the poor boy's head at a press conference.

I made all the right noises in public about the shocking duplicity of some people attempting to extort money from celebrities, while privately paying the actress and her son a small fortune to disappear. The press and the public soon forgot the minor scandal, turning their attention elsewhere. Not my mum. She was like a dog with a bone between its teeth.

My dad, my poor henpecked dad, also lived off my mother's castrating largesse while occupying a top-floor office in his wife's tower block with a purely figurehead title attached to the door. That sign was screwed and so was dad. At first, he'd tried to input ideas at board-room level but no one, especially mum, took any notice. As the realization hit home that it was just a way in which his wife could keep an eye on him, he learned to play golf, spending most of his day on the links or else at the nineteenth hole.

When that became too much he would retire to the basement office he's set up in their home to natter with his mates or else fashion superb wooden objects with his own hands. He began selling his items on the net, garnering not only a little welcome extra cash for himself but also a great deal of personal satisfaction. When I asked him once why he didn't do it for a living, he admitted, "Too lazy, son. If I did it because I had to, it would suck the joy right out of it. This way I do it when the mood strikes and it keeps me happy."

My apartment contains one of his greatest constructions; an intricately carved and polished armoire which has pride of place in the bedroom. Many of those friends and acquaintances of mine who have seen it have coveted the piece so I referred them to my dad who eventually made a tidy sum manufacturing furniture for the cognoscenti. My mum also loves it and attempted to wrest control of it from me as she despises the bland uniformity of closets. When I told her it was not for sale at any price but that all she had to do was ask her husband to make her one, she laughed out loud at the idea that my father could possibly manufacture anything at all, let alone such a work of beauty. She believed I lied because I didn't want anyone else to share my good fortune.

"She's on the warpath, son. Your brother, Peter, has been encouraging her. He's up to his eyeballs in gambling debts and he desperately needs your mum to bail him out."

Peter was my younger brother. He was blessed with good-looks, a smarmy personality, a wit based on belittling those less fortunate which meant just about everyone, plus the one thing that I was sadly lacking: heterosexuality. He stuck his dick into any hole that moved, as long as it was female, while I allowed any cock that got hard to stick itself into any of my warm, wet holes. Or I did until I fell in love with Gavin.

I can't say we were totally faithful but when we strayed it was usually together and we didn't do it often. Best way to explain it: we didn't go looking but if it fell into our laps, we didn't usually turn it down.

"Dad, she's always on the warpath when it comes to me. Nothing short of marriage and a legion of kids will satisfy her and then she'd find fault because they weren't good-looking enough for her standards. She's the basis for all those Gothic novels where the wife keeps her husband or his previous wife locked in the attic because they're too ugly or too stupid or too not to her liking."

Dad laughed. I knew he loved her although he found it increasingly difficult to tolerate her controlling ways. On a few occasions, he'd even fled the nest to spend a few days rest and recuperation with Gavin and me, happy in our spare room. He knew of our relationship and approved. He would have approved of whoever made his son happy, be it human, animal, vegetable or mineral.

"This time it's serious, Chad. She intends sparking a confrontation with you. Peter has been spurring her on over the past few weeks after that debacle about your child. What were you thinking?"

"I guess I wasn't, dad."

"Just tell her the truth, Chad. She'll come around. Eventually. And if she doesn't, then she doesn't deserve a son like you."

"Can't afford the truth, dad."

"I'll help out as best I can."

"Thanks for the offer. Really."

Dad sighed down the line. "What she's cooked up, mainly at Peter's instigation, is so twisted even I can't believe she'll go through with it."

I laughed. "Something so evil that she's setting me up to fail?"

By the time dad had explained the plan, the smile had been well and truly wiped from my face. Mum's plan, with obvious input from Peter, was more than evil; it was diabolical.

"In a way, I'm sorry I told you son. Maybe it's time she faced up to the truth."

"That would mean me having to face up to poverty, dad. Tried that once when I was younger. Didn't like it. Not really me. I actually like to have three meals a day and live in something more substantial than a cardboard box."

"What will you do?"

"I'll just have to fake it somehow. I'll think of something."

"If she suspects there's even a remote possibility you're faking it then she'll have a contingency plan."

"Thanks for the warning, dad. That gives me a couple of hours to plan."

"Don't forget to act surprised."

"I'll be so woefully unprepared for her visit, she won't suspect a thing."

Dad chuckled, knowing my love of theatricals. "Just be thankful I overheard their plans, otherwise you would have been up shit creek without a paddle."

I was anyway. Even if the number of hours between the warning and my mother's arrival had doubled or tripled I don't believe I could have come up with a plan to thwart her and my brother. I was fucked, and not in a nice way. Gavin and I were just going to have to adapt to circumstances. What if my dad had been set up? What if mum knew he was eavesdropping and fed him a line, planning something even more diabolical in its place? We couldn't go there.

Thank the fates that mum lived an entire coast away because it gave us time to prepare. Had she lived in the next state there would have been no time at all. I was a nervous wreck by the time she buzzed the door. I feigned a nonchalance I definitely didn't feel as I opened the door.

Deep gasp of surprise. "Mum, what are you doing here?"

Give her time to take in the fluffy slippers and the flamboyant Chinese silk dressing gown. Unable to hide her distaste at my sartorial choices she was obviously satisfied that I had not been forewarned of her arrival. It was my coup de théâtre. I knew she would suspect something had I attempted to butch it up. Better to play it as naturally as possible.

"Would you like some breakfast, mother?"

"Chad, it's after midday. Normal people have been up for hours."

I didn't like the way she emphasized 'normal.'

"I had a hectic party to attend last night. I didn't get home until the wee hours of the morn." I rattled off a few names of the glitterati that I knew would impress her.

"I suppose you went with that creature you call your bodyguard?"

"Then you suppose incorrectly. Gavin does have his own social life."

I lied brazenly hoping she would not bother to check.

Her response was sarcasm. "You do surprise me, Chadwick. I thought the two of you were glued at the hip. Or somewhere of a more intimate nature."

"Mother. Your mind is in the sewer."

"Where, if rumor is to be believed, you have been residing for some time."

"I thought you of all people would know better than to believe rumor." She had been on the receiving end of a particularly nasty smear as a young woman. It had been a fabrication but that wasn't revealed until her reputation had suffered a great deal of harm.

"May I use your bathroom? It's been a long journey and I need to freshen up."

"Of course."

Before I could steer her to the main bathroom which I kept blandly functional for guests, she'd headed for the en suite off my bedroom. Just before she closed the bedroom door to cut off the sound of her sticky-beaking in my armoire and my bathroom cabinets, she called cheerily over her shoulder, "Oh, be a dear. When Sharon gets here, show her a good time."

She closed the door on my startled, "Who's Sharon?"

I knew exactly who, or rather what, Sharon was but my look of surprise was genuine. I simply could not believe my mother would stoop to such depths, even goaded there by my brother. I suspect my mother's desire for respectability made her and my brother equal partners in this sleazy scheme.

I didn't have long to think it over because mere seconds after I heard mum lock the bedroom door, the apartment door buzzer shattered my thoughts. I would have liked to change but I was stuck with my screaming queen outfit. Oh well, I'd make the most of it. Pasting the most welcoming smile on my face, I opened the door, took in the woman standing there and beamed, "You must be Sharon?" to which she replied with an equally appalling fake smile, "You must be Chadwick. Your mother has told me so much about you."

She managed to keep a straight face as she looked me up and down, her heart clearly sinking as she recognized campery when she saw it. She couldn't keep the edge of humor out of her voice when she said, "Nice outfit."

Before I stood aside to allow her to enter, I whispered, "She is currently in my bedroom and I'd be willing to bet my entire collection of Ken dolls that she's listening to our every word, so if we play our parts right we may just get through this with our dignity intact."

If I hadn't been watching her mouth I may not have noticed the wry manner in which the edges of her lips curled up at my suggestion. There was hope we could work this out.

Sharon entered, giving what she could see of the apartment the once over. She must have liked what she saw. The apartment no longer screamed 'queen' because Gavin and I had had enough time to remove the most obvious items such as gay porn DVDs and various other artifacts of gay erotica. The artworks now were more in keeping with my genuine interest in Mesoamerican art and sculpture.

After I'd poured us both a crisp dry white wine – Sharon knew her grapes which was something in her favor – we sat on the lounge pretending a friendship neither of us felt as we circled each other psychologically in an attempt to find a weak spot. I was not supposed to know what she was here for so it gave me a slight advantage. I discovered much to my chagrin, that under normal circumstances I could quite possibly have got to like Sharon. We chatted amiably for almost twenty minutes while my mother rifled through my personal effects in the bedroom in a futile attempt to find anything incriminating.

The sound of her banging drawers closed or slamming doors made her frustration all the more delicious. Sharon studied me carefully as we heard an explosive curse from behind the locked door. Recognition seemed to animate her face before she quickly subdued it.

"You know, don't you?" she smiled.

"That my mother is turning my bedroom and my medicine cabinet upside down in a vain attempt to discover I'm gay?" I nodded. "Amongst other things."

"You know about me, too?"

I wasn't prepared to admit prior knowledge just yet. "I think I can take a pretty good guess. You don't know my mother at all. You didn't pick up on the few strategically placed bogus items about her past when I introduced them in conversation which led me to believe that you are comparatively recent acquaintances. Therefore, I deduced you were brought along today to give your opinion as to whether you believe I bat for the opposing team, to seduce me, or attempt to insinuate yourself into my social group."

She fidgeted as if she wanted to be anywhere but on the lounge with me. "Much worse than that, I'm afraid."

"How did you get yourself caught up in this mess?"

"Student," she said simply. "Tuition fees, books, rent."

I nodded my head to show that I understood.

She grabbed her bag and stood up. "Look, you seem like a really nice guy. I don't care whether you're gay or straight, or any other permutation for that matter. I think what your mother is doing is sick. I don't want any part of it."

"She must be paying a bucketload of money. Enough to cover the job plus enough to anaesthetize your conscience."

She laughed. "You know your mother well."

"Why not stick around, see how it all turns out?"

"I'm warning you, there'll be tears before bedtime."

"As long as they're not mine. I hope you got your money up front?"

"Mmmm. Half up front as a deposit. Half when the job is completed. A substantial bonus if I get the result she wants."

I was about to assure her it was all right but mother took that moment to finally come back into the living room, her face ablaze. I'm sure she would have approached the entire matter in a much more subtle manner had she discovered even a skerrick of evidence one way or the other in her search.

"I heard you admiring my armoire, mother. I hope you put everything back as you found it."

My attitude set her off and running. "I hope you and Sharon have been having a nice little chat."

"We have," I said while Sharon nodded her head nervously. "She is obviously not a friend of long standing so I wondered if she's coming to work for you, if she's the daughter of a friend, or—"

Mother snapped. "Don't be obtuse, Chad. She's here to fuck your brains out to prove to my satisfaction once and for all that you're..." she screwed up her face in distaste, "...gay."

"That's really sweet, mother, but perhaps if you wanted to prove to yourself that I was gay you could simply have asked."

"What would you have said?"

"That it was none of your goddam business. It also seems somewhat odd to me that you would bring a woman over to, as you so quaintly put it, fuck my brains out to prove I'm gay when an oiled truck driver with big muscles seems a much better option."

Sharon snorted quietly into her wine.

"I have no intention of paying for your queer boys. Besides, I want to see if there's any hope for you."

"Hope for you is if I screw Sharon?"

"Of course."

"If I refuse?"

"Then I'll know you're a filthy queer. I'll cut you off without a penny."

"You'll give it all to my worthless brother Peter who will gamble away your company within a year."

She shrieked. I must have hit a raw nerve. "That's not true. He's seeking professional help."

"Like last time and the time before."

"This is not about Peter, this is about you."

I stood up abruptly, my hand on my belt. "So, how are we to do this, mother? Here on the floor in front of you? Or do you have a movie camera in your bag so Sharon and I can discreetly adjourn to the bedroom where we consummate your hope for my future, capturing it in glorious color? Or is it to be projected onto the television here in the living room so you can watch your older son shove his cock into a hired pussy."

Mother looked somewhat rattled. I decided to press my advantage.

"Let's stop all the bullshit, shall we? I'll just get my dick out right here so you can watch Sharon go down on me, mum. Then I'll lick her cunt a little, finger her clit until I've got her writhing, and then ram my cock inside her, ride her like a cowboy rides a steer until I plant my seed deep inside her cunt. Will that prove my bona fides, eh?"

I began to unzip and pull my trousers down over my legs.

Sharon was horrified, my mother crimson with embarrassment.

"Stop it!" my mother yelled. "How vulgar and common you've become."

I was flabbergasted. "Me? I'm not the one who's paying a student to fuck me to prove something. Anyway, we can fake it. Did you think of that? Eh?"

The look on Sharon's face revealed she had.

With a look of utmost triumph on her face, my mother produced a pair of rubber gloves from her handbag as well as a small syringe, a number of cotton swabs and enough medical paraphernalia for a small operation.

"Oh, dear Lord, tell me that's not what it looks like."

"Well, smart ass, go on, tell me what it looks like."

My mother's audacity knocked the wind out of my sails. "Are you really going to examine Sharon's cunt for traces of my sperm?" I shook my head in disgust. "And you're going to take a swab to test the DNA to ensure it's my sperm?"

I should have put an end to the farce at that point but the afternoon had reached its own crazy momentum and it was difficult to stop. Grabbing Sharon by the hand, I dragged her into the bedroom, slamming and locking the door behind me.

Sharon sat on the bed and immediately got an attack of the giggles. "I thought *my* mother was a bitch. Oh, sorry."

"Go ahead. Be my guest. Say what you like about mine, it won't even approach how base she is." I flopped down on the bed beside her. "How are we going to go about doing this?"

My question wiped the smile off her face. "You're not gay?"

"Look at me love. Have you ever seen a gayer man?"

"Without meaning to be rude about it, no one would ever mistake you for straight."

"I don't think it's rude to point out the bleedin' obvious."

"But you want to try?"

"Not really. I don't think a vagina is going to get me hard."

"I could…like…um…play with it or maybe give it a suck. Perhaps if I turned the light off, closed the curtains."

I shrugged my indifference. "I'm the one that usually gets fucked, you see. I don't get hard unless I have something wedged in my ass."

Sharon was trying to be helpful. "I could use my fingers." When that suggestion didn't seem to have the effect she was after, she tried again. "Maybe there's something in the bathroom we can use, like the handle of a hair brush or a roll-on deodorant container."

There was a sharp knock on the bedroom door. "You've got forty-five minutes to come up with the goods. Then I'm off," my mother called.

"A deadline is always conducive to getting a good result," I snickered.

"Look, I don't mind at all walking away right now. She's paid me half and it's a tidy sum. It'll tide me over for a month or so. That way you'll have your dignity."

"But no inheritance."

"Yes, I keep forgetting that."

I decided to press my case. "Look, are you on my side in this?"

"Hell, yes."

"Then pop into the bathroom and strip off. There's a dressing gown behind the door, wear that. Okay? Knock when you're ready to come out."

Once she'd disappeared I went to the armoire and ran my fingers across the solid timber back until I found the lever. I pulled it down and the false back popped open revealing the entrance to the Panic Room Gavin and I had installed when we first moved in. I tapped gently in code. The door opened and Gavin came out of his hiding place. We'd stored all the incriminating evidence inside along with my own boyfriend. He swept me into his arms, kissing me passionately. He slipped out of his clothes and covered himself with the sheet and the blankets on the bed. I stripped and joined him after I'd lowered the lights.

A few minutes later, Sharon tapped on the bathroom door and I called for her to come in. I wondered what she thought when she saw me in the bed waiting for her. She didn't appear at all shy and shucked the dressing gown, openly displaying her body before slipping into the bed beside me. I'd rumpled the blankets so Gavin remained hidden.

She tried to encourage me. "We can take this as fast or as slow as you like."

"Open your legs," I instructed quietly.

She lay on her back and parted her legs. I tweaked her nipples and squeezed her tits but my cock remained resolutely limp until I felt Gavin's hand secretly caress my balls. I ducked my head under the bedclothes tracing my fingers across Sharon's stomach stopping just short of her landscaped pubic region. Gavin took over from there as I watched in the near darkness. Running his fingers along her slit, he thumbed the folds aside to rub her clit forcing a moan from Sharon's lips. He pushed his middle finger into her cunt, extracting it to show me how wet she was. He sucked it clean then pushed in for more. He added another finger and pushed in gently varying the angle for greater pleasure. I watched mesmerized as his fingers disappeared into her pussy that was so slick with juice. She still seemed oblivious to the fact there were two men in the bed with her.

Gavin inched his way between her legs while I kept away from her lest our subterfuge be discovered. He breathed on to her cunt lips before extending his tongue to lick along the folds until he could wrap his lips around her clit. He sucked as he pushed his fingers inside her then swapped so his tongue poked where his fingers had been as they now rubbed her button. Her breath was irregular as Gavin buried his face between her thighs sucking and licking as she neared orgasm. I'm afraid I found the sight of my boyfriend using his mouth on a woman a complete turn on and my cock hardened against my stomach.

Sharon wrapped her legs around Gavin's head holding him in place as she ground her pussy against his mouth. She thrashed about in the throes of orgasm as I finally bobbed my head out of the sheet to gasp for fresh air. I whipped the bedclothes off her to reveal Gavin, his face slick with her juices, bringing her off.

She was wide-eyed at the revelation.

"Holy fuck," she panted, "No wonder that was so intense." She reached down to squeeze my cock. "What have we here? Someone's not as averse to women as he thought."

"Nah, it's watching my boyfriend sucking your cunt that turned me on."

"No matter, you're hard."

Unfortunately, even as she spoke, my cock began to deflate. Gavin must have realized what I needed and reached for my limp prick. The difference in touch was amazing and I was hard again in seconds.

"Suck me, Chad. Get me ready."

I kneeled to take Gavin in my mouth.

"Dear mother of God," Sharon gasped when she saw the size of Gavin's cock. "I thought yours was big, Chad, but his is gigantic."

I smirked. "Tell me about it."

Sharon wriggled to sit up against the headboard so she could watch as I took Gavin's prick in my mouth. After years of practice I had little trouble accommodating it my throat. My lover had a smooth action and knew just how far and how hard to thrust so that I wouldn't gag. I got his weapon nice and slick before I relinquished my hold over him.

"Your turn," I said to Sharon. She scrambled eagerly to get at the monster and I must admit I was pleased that her first efforts resulted in her choking, drool running out the corners of her mouth. By the time she had adjusted and was taking Gavin's cock almost as expertly as I did, it was time for the next course.

Gavin reared up on his knees, aiming his cock at Sharon's drooling slit. I helped guide it to its target, holding his balls as he slid slowly into her cunt, stretching the lips until they clung to his shaft as he pistoned in and out. Her mouth hung open in pleasure and Gavin honed in with his tongue. I stroked myself as I watched his ass bob up and down, jamming his cock all the way to his balls.

I knew Gavin was bisexual when we began our relationship but he'd never expressed a desire for cunt in the years we'd been together. However, he didn't turn down the option when I'd come up with my plan to defeat my mum at her own game. Sharon clawed his back with her nails as he pounded her into the mattress, her groans loud enough to be heard in the living room. I guessed mum would think Sharon was playacting but I didn't care. All I knew was I was hot as hell and needed to dump a load. But there was only one orifice that would do the trick to prove to my mother that I was a 'man.' Her definition of a man, not mine.

I recognized the sounds Gavin was making and moved my face down to that unknown area between Sharon's legs waiting to receive my reward. "Are you ready, babe?" Gavin gasped.

"Give it to me, lover," I replied.

Gavin withdrew his cock, slick with his own pre-cum and Sharon's own orgasm, plunged his prick into my mouth so that I tasted their mingled juices, and shot his load down the back of my throat. My cock was fit to burst as I tasted Gavin, feeling his spunk run down into my gullet.

I was hard as iron. I didn't think about what I had to do. Aiming my cock at Sharon's cunt, I pushed into her squishy hole. It wasn't an ass which I had been known to fuck on occasions, but it wasn't half bad, even though it was not an experience I was likely to repeat. Not knowing how long my cock would stay hard without other stimulus, Gavin rammed his still slick fingers between my butt cheeks and into my boy cunt. That did it!

I'm nowhere near as big as Gavin in the cock department but I'm no slouch either, measuring above the average range. I noticed Sharon had closed her eyes and was doing her best to prolong her pleasure. As I was getting into the swing of it, a bit carried away with my own dexterity, I slammed into her pussy, feeling my balls clutch ready to empty themselves into the unfamiliar wetness.

The wail began slowly until Sharon was begging me to fuck her hard, to bring her off. I didn't know how to oblige other than to pound her pussy harder while I did my best to stave off my orgasm. Then Sharon shuddered, her pussy muscles clamping around my cock as I shot my wad deep into her as she continued to orgasm beneath me.

It was probably ungentlemanly of me, but I withdrew as soon as I knew I'd deposited enough spunk inside her. Gavin substituted his fingers until she collapsed satiated and satisfied. I thought a certain degree of embarrassment may have resulted from our threesome but instead it was the giggles that predominated. Then I thought of what came next: the total humiliation when my mother donned her Tweetie Pie yellow rubber gloves to score a sample of my semen from Sharon's puffy cunt. Suddenly, I found the idea utterly repellent.

"You know what? Let's not do this."

Sharon was surprised. "After all you went through to ensure your allowance?"

"It's your decision, babe," Gavin said, kissing me gently on the cheek.

Wrapping the dressing gown around me, tying it tight so there was no way my private bits would be on show; I unlocked the bedroom door and swaggered into the living room. My mother looked up smirking.

"I hope you're pleased with yourself, mum," I spat. "I did it. Just as you asked. I fucked a woman in the cunt. It was the first time. It's likely to be the last. Not because I found it repulsive or anything like that. Quite the contrary. But you see I prefer to take cock up my ass. Yeah, I'm gay as a goose and twice as frisky. Come on in to the bedroom, mum. I'd like you to meet someone."

My mother's curiosity turned to shock when she saw the naked bodies of Sharon and Gavin lying exhausted on the bed.

"You don't have to believe me, mum, but that's my spunk you can see glistening in the folds of Sharon's cunt. That's Gavin beside her. He's my PA, my bodyguard, and the man I have loved more than anyone in the world for the past two years. The only way I could get hard enough to fuck Sharon was to watch him in action first, then copy his technique while his fingers were wedged up my ass. In case you're interested, he's bi, but prefers to spend his time fucking me. I consider myself the luckiest guy in the world."

For once in my life my mother was too shocked to say anything.

"Now, unless you want to watch young Gavin there plough my ass while I scream like the nelly queen I am, I suggest you take your rubber gloves, your swabs and your pissy attitude and fuck off."

My mother was out the apartment door faster than a Tour de France champ on drugs.

Turning to Sharon, I apologized sheepishly. "I'll get your money for you, don't worry. I'm sorry you were put through all that. I should have had the balls to say what I just did at the beginning, not at the end."

"I don't regret it one bit," Sharon said patting Gavin's prick with what looked like longing. "I'll just grab a shower if you don't mind."

"Leave your phone number so we know where to find you."

Instead of using the en suite, Sharon headed for the main bathroom down the hall, taking her clothes with her.

Gavin swept me in his arms. "You were so brave telling the old trout off like that. I was hoping you'd do it one day."

"I feel awful that I kept you a secret for so long. Can you forgive me?"

"Nothing to forgive."

"Fuck me, Gavin."

"With pleasure, babe."

Hoisting my legs onto his shoulders, he reached to the bedside table to retrieve the lube we always kept there. Squeezing a gob onto his fingers, he massaged it into my hole before slicking his cock which was rampant again.

"So, we're like an item now?" he asked as he prodded at my entrance.

"Definitely."

He slid into me, his cock parting my sphincter muscles in one fluid motion.

"In that case," he said as he increased the pressure inside me. "How about we make it official?"

"How?"

"Will you marry me?"

There's no way in the world I could ever turn down a guy who had his huge cock pressed against my prostate as I whimpered for more.

Bi One,
Get One Free

"For Heaven's sake, Alex, when are you going to come out at work? Aren't you sick of making up stories about your non-existent girlfriend?"

"She's not non-existent," Alex wailed. "She's you."

"I am not now nor have I ever been your girlfriend."

Melanie knew Alex would be smiling now even though he was on the other end of her cell phone. "There was that time you got pissed at the Christmas party and you were all over me like the proverbial rash. You even had your hand down the front of my pants." She was right; she could hear the smile in his voice. He never left off accusing her of molesting him.

"If you weren't interested, why did you have an erection?" She thought the question was reasonable.

"All my cock knew was that it was being fondled, it doesn't care who is doing it. Does your pussy know the sex of the fingers being pushed inside it?"

Their argument always progressed along the same lines. Neither was willing to concede an inch as to who started it. To the delight of some and the disgust of others, Melanie and Alex had been tongue pashing on the lounge in a state of alcoholic arousal for a good fifteen minutes before Melanie went for the grope. Truth been known she'd wanted Alex deep inside her ever since they'd first met. She had a voracious appetite for cock — it was something they had in common. Alex had a definite preference for the bottom role when he made it with hot men.

His interest in women as sexual partners was minimal; non-existent really. He liked Melanie – but not like that. The kissing had been fine, he had no problem with kissing his best female friend even when she pushed her tongue far enough into his mouth that he almost choked. Most of his boyfriends had been woeful in the kissing department so he was pleased to get in some practice. A kiss is a kiss, after all, the only difference being the beard rash.

He hadn't even minded when she put her hand around his cock inside his trousers and began to gently jerk him off. In fact, he'd been close to unzipping his fly to give her better access, totally oblivious to the fact they were in full view of everyone at the party. Alex merely overlaid the female hand with a masculine fantasy and as it had been over a week since he'd blown his load, he didn't care one way or the other. Horniness is no respecter of gender.

The whole experimental enterprise had collapsed like a flimsy house of cards when Melanie had placed Alex's hand over her mound and guided his fingers into her pussy. She was wet with anticipation but the moment Alex felt his digits sink into the 'squishiness' as he called it, it was all over. He was neither sexist nor a misogynist but his brain rebelled, quickly deflating his cock. It was as if someone had thrown a bucket of cold water over him.

Melanie had backtracked quickly without releasing his rapidly deflating prick but the moment had passed.

It was enough to convince most of Alex's coworkers that he was a libertine from whom their wives and girlfriends were unsafe, and convince management of the firm that Alex was an exhibitionist and couldn't hold his grog. He found himself shunned and his career stalled. That had been eight months ago.

Melanie knew how important this latest company party was. It was Alex's attempt to lay the unsavory rumors to rest. If he turned up with the same girlfriend it would allay the fears of those who believed he was rampantly promiscuous and, if he was on his best behavior, it would show the boss and his cohorts that last year's display was a drunken aberration. Of course, Alex could come out of the closet at work but he feared that was a solution too radical for Rodgers, Coplan & Blaine. Conservatism, reliability, steadfastness, adherence to the old ways; those were the values you signed up for when you joined the company. If you rocked the boat, chances are everyone would be pitched into the waves and drowned. Steady as she goes was the best way.

It was all bullshit, of course. Everyone in the company knew that but it didn't pay to show your contempt for the social niceties. That's why Alex toed the company line. It's why his life was tangled up with so many lies that he could scarcely keep track of them and it was why he needed one constant to which he could return when things went ass up. Like now.

Melanie had heard it all before. She was tired of playing beard to his closetedness. She'd hoped with his new boyfriend he'd find the courage to come out so he could live his love openly. No such luck. He'd hammered himself so tightly inside the closet he was in real danger of suffocation.

Besides, she was pissed off that she'd been neglected of late. Every time Alex thought he'd found the love of his life, he disappeared from hers; sometimes for weeks at a time. She understood that initial period where you only have eyes for each other, where nothing in the world matters but the object of your affection. She'd even felt it herself once or twice, but Alex made it a habit. If she were honest with herself, she missed his daily calls and their lunches at which they gossiped about the latest movie star scandals or who among their friends was sleeping with whom. Then the relationship was over before the initial limerance had even settled and Alex would be back on the phone as if nothing had happened, as if they'd been speaking just the previous day instead of two months ago.

That's what had happened this time. Little contact except a late night call from an excited Alex to say he'd just seen the man he was going to spend the rest of his life with. The 'rest of my life' to Alex was a variable, usually lasting from overnight to a number of weeks. She had no reason to think the current infatuation would be any different with…what was his name?

So, she wasn't surprised when she got the frantic call about the firm's party to find that Alex was on the phone asking her to be his date. No, begging her. She wasn't going to make it easy on him this time. Maybe she could even blackmail him: that he'd let her blow him in exchange for her 'performance' as his girlfriend. She was careful to word it so it could be brushed off as a joke. At heart, she didn't want to jeopardize their friendship no matter how much she felt Alex was taking advantage of her kindness.

"Ewww," Alex said down the phone. "Don't even go there."

She wasn't about to let him off the hook that easily. "We could go to your favorite glory hole and you could stick it through the wall. You won't even know it's me."

She could hear how much Alex was squirming by the sound of his voice. Plus the fact he totally disregarded what she had just suggested. "Look, I don't have time to argue. Will you or won't you be my date tonight?"

"It's extremely short notice. I'll have to rearrange things with a few people," she lied. Mel had kept the night free. She always entered important dates in Alex's life in her diary because she knew she would receive the frantic phone call at the last minute and she would always make herself available. She knew that and Alex knew that but they always played these games before she finally capitulated. Otherwise she would have felt like a door mat.

Deep down, she knew the only thing that complicated Alex's life was Alex himself. If he just manned up and admitted he was gay, she was sure everything would work out fine.

"Will you or won't you?"

Mel could hear Alex was getting impatient. Time to end the charade.

"Yes, Alex, I will, seeing as you asked so nicely." She grabbed a pen and piece of paper to write down the details. She added a rider. "Alex, this is the last time. I mean it."

They both knew she said that every time it happened. One of these days, Mel thought, I really will mean it.

Alex ground his teeth. Nothing was going right for him this evening. He'd taken longer than usual to convince Mel to be his date. She sounded particularly pissed off. More so than usual. Okay, he hadn't been in contact as regularly as normal but, hey, even best friends needed some breathing space from time to time. He relied on her. He'd always been there for her. Not that she'd ever asked him anything as devious and underhanded as he'd asked of her on…how many times had she played the role of his girlfriend now? It didn't matter. That's what friends were for, wasn't it?

When this was over, he'd take her out to one of those really expensive restaurants she was always reading about in those crappy social magazines that she used as fodder for her fantasy life. He and his new boyfriend, Dario, would take her.

He slapped the steering wheel of his car in frustration. "Damn." He wasn't sure he had a 'new boyfriend' any longer. They'd parted under anything but happy circumstances earlier. It was the reason Alex was running late and had had to beg Mel to make her own way to the party telling her he'd meet her there. Then a flat battery in his car had added another forty minutes to his delay.

"Mel hates people who don't turn up on time," he muttered to himself.

He hoped she wouldn't give up and leave the party. So much depended on her being there. He'd rung the house, offering apologies for his car. He couldn't believe his bad luck when Lanyon Blaine, one of the firm's partners answered the phone. Lanyon was a notorious office sleaze who, it was rumored, had bedded half the female staff. He had often complimented Alex on his good taste in dating Melissa so it pained Alex to ask him to keep an eye on her so she didn't feel neglected, especially when Lanyon's response had been laced with innuendo. Alex had earlier received the chilliest of receptions from Mel herself when he rang to explain the circumstances for his late appearance. It wasn't his fault that he had mechanical problem.

It also wasn't his fault that Dario was proving to be a bastard; making totally unreasonable demands on their relationship.

"Enough! You have to come out at work, Alex," he'd shouted. "I want to be your date when you go to these company parties. I refuse to be locked in the closet with you. My last boyfriend did that. I won't let it happen again. You need to make up your mind. Next time you take me or it's all over."

Alex never reacted well to demands. Not those sort anyway. Life wasn't just black and white as Dario liked to insist. There were all those lovely shades of grey. It was among charcoal, night sky, woodland grey, shale, baby seal, thunderstorm that he felt most at home. Not so either of the people who meant most to him in the world.

"Fuck," he swore, hitting the steering wheel again.

"Just let me get through tonight. I'll think it over in the morning," he promised any of the Fates who may have been listening at that moment. There was enough stress involved with this evening's subterfuge without the other pressures on him.

He really would sit himself down and attempt to work out his life tomorrow, although he'd probably be too hung over and lethargic; exhausted from all the effort required that evening. Perhaps, the day after would be a better time to consider his options.

There, he was doing it again. He hated making important decisions. There was something so final about them. You couldn't take them back if you'd made a mistake.

Like tonight. It had been a mistake for Alex to drop in on Dario on his way to the party, but he wanted to see the new man in his life. He missed him. He did regret that he couldn't take Dario with him. He would have liked nothing better than to show off his deeply tanned, darkly Mediterranean boyfriend to his co-workers. Mind you, he didn't know whether the company would permit him to acknowledge Dario as his partner; no one had ever tested those waters. Alex was too much the coward to be the first.

That's what had caused the worst disagreement he'd ever had with Dario. Alex accepted his boyfriend was hot-blooded; that's what he liked most about him. Dario, however, was not only passionate in bed but equally as passionate in his beliefs. The major sticking point in their relationship, in which Dario was in agreement with Mel, was that Alex needed to come out at work.

Dario and Alex could not keep their hands off one another. Even when Alex turned up at the door in his best dinner suit, immaculate in his grooming and adamant in his decision to go to the party with Mel, it hadn't stopped the sparks which ended with Alex on his knees, fully dressed, sucking for dear life on Dario's thick drooling prick, his boyfriend messing up his expensive coiffure. He weighed it up in his mind: hair versus cock. Cock won every time.

That was until Dario began whining again about being invited to the party. Alex felt he had to stand up for himself so there were constant interruptions to giving head. Alex got progressively angrier and his blow job equally belligerent until he scraped the head of Dario's prodigious cock with his teeth.

Dario's reaction was immediate and unexpected. "You know what?" he spat. "Let's just forget it." For emphasis, he zipped up his fly. "Go to this party that means more to you than I do. Take your pretend girlfriend. When you get yourself a pair of balls, give me a ring. There's a small chance I might still be available."

Alex stormed out after brushing the grime from the knees of his dinner trousers. He glanced in the rear vision mirror now that he was nearing his destination in another vain attempt to pat down the strands of hair that stuck up like spikes after Dario had run his hands through it.

"Bugger." No amount of spit had any effect. He also looked down at the wet spots on his shirt where he'd attempted, also with a similar lack of success, to remove a few grease spots that had spattered when he'd attempted to work out why his car simply refused to work. It was almost as if fate wanted to stop him from attending the function. Everyone, even inanimate objects, was conspiring against him.

To make matters worse still, he was horny as fuck. Dario's uncompleted blow job left him feeling empty. His mouth itched for cock, his ass itched for cock, even his cock itched for cock. When he was in a mood like this he was agitated, he was irritated, he would be like a funnel web spider with a sore head until he did something about it. He probably should have pulled off to a secluded spot on the side of the road and taken himself in hand. It was a stop-gap measure but it would have tided him over. Now he was driving into the car park at the mansion where the party was taking place. All right, the first thing he'd do before seeking out Mel was to find a toilet to flush his anger and his horniness down the u-bend where it belonged. Then he would do his best to endure the evening before taking himself home to work through his mountain of problems, not least of which would be repairing his relationship with Dario.

It proved easier thought than done. The downstairs toilets, and they were numerous, had long lines waiting to use them. Alex didn't have the time or the patience. If he had to wait much longer he'd probably attack one of the hot men he worked with. He eyed the velvet rope barrier excluding partygoers from the upstairs. That meant he'd find relief up there. He loitered nearby keeping an eye open for a chance to disappear upstairs unseen. When the opportunity arose, he was just ducking under the rope when who should be descending the staircase but Lanyon Blaine.

"That rope is there for a reason, Alex," Lanyon sneered. At least his boss hadn't used his family name; that would have meant real trouble. Informality was the keyword for the evening.

There was no love lost between the two men.

"Look, Lanyon, I'm in desperate need of the men's room. There's a waiting list a mile long for all the downstairs facilities." Alex bobbed about on the balls of his feet for emphasis. Unfortunately, that drew Lanyon's attention to his crotch, the outline of his rampant cock clearly visible in his tight trousers.

Lanyon was in no hurry to relieve Alex's embarrassment. In fact, he meant to prolong it. "Looks like your girlfriend is not putting out enough, Alex. You got blue balls? You have to understand, if I allow you upstairs then what's to stop everyone asking?"

Alex wasn't in the mood to argue, he probably would have said things he regretted later to the smug bastard blocking his way, so he turned on his heels to find somewhere private to relieve his stress.

"Come on, Alex. I was playing with you. I can't leave a fellow with that sort of problem in his pants. You'll scare the women at the party. All the proper ones, at least. From the size of that thing, you'll have the improper ones salivating, and we can't have that, either. Too much competition for me."

Vain bastard. Still, Alex was thankful he'd changed his mind, no matter the reason. He followed Lanyon up the stairs and along a tastefully decorated hallway until he opened the door on a bathroom that was equal in size to Alex's living room. "There you go," he said. "Take your time."

Alex muttered his thanks, for he was grateful. He went to lock the door to avoid interruptions but Lanyon had followed him into the bathroom, closing the door behind him, sliding the bolt across.

"There, now we won't be disturbed."

"What are you doing?" Alex asked, backing away from Lanyon, praying he didn't intend joining him in his masturbatory fantasies. Lanyon was built and buff but he was also Alex's boss. Those are the combustible ingredients for a very short career.

Lanyon slowly lowered the fly to his trousers before hauling out a delicious looking cock and pair of balls. Alex stared at his tackle mesmerized.

The oppressive silence was broken when Lanyon nodded at his cock, and said, "I heard a rumor that you're a fag, Alex."

Melissa was bored off her face. The alcohol was doing nothing to improve her mood. She'd tried joining a few of the groups conversing around the various rooms but she'd quickly tired of their mundane preoccupations and their office politics. Life was so much more than that. She'd even asked a handful of the more attractive men to dance, to the jealous snarls of their wives and girlfriends who proved an insurmountable impediment.

The only bright spot in an otherwise pissy evening was Lanyon Blaine's efforts to entertain her supposedly on Alex's instructions. She would have used the word 'detain' because she was convinced Alex believed she would leave out of sheer ill-will or utter boredom before he arrived. It was a toss-up as to which reason she would use because both were true. Lanyon had proved to be a rather delicious distraction. She knew he was married. She also knew of his reputation; Alex had warned her, but there was something charismatic to the man. Sure, he was handsome as fuck and his body seemed shaped like any girl's wet dream beneath his smart formal wear. He also had an easy charm that would work a treat on bored wives or neglected girlfriends. It just wasn't going to work on her, unless…

She'd been at the party for over an hour and if Alex didn't turn up soon she'd cut loose. There would be worse ways to spend a little time than with Lanyon embedded in her pussy. She was already incredibly wet from Lanyon dancing so close she could feel his strong erection pressed against her body. That action made her aware of what she was missing out on. He wouldn't be her first choice if she could find someone better. She glanced around the room after begging off another dance with the octopus-armed Lanyon whose hands always seemed to be in spots they shouldn't. She was exhausted from moving them after her requests fell on deaf ears.

Most of the men were 'taken' and those singles that weren't were of such limited appeal that her vibrator had more personality. Wait, when did *he* arrive? She hadn't noticed him before. God, he was sex on legs. At least what she could see of him. Some of the single women from Alex's firm had bailed him up but she couldn't see any of the women clutching at his hand possessively. Nor, from her vantage point, could she see a woman watching him like a hawk. Either, he had a very easygoing girlfriend or he was a new member of the company staff. Either way, she was determined to find out.

Waiting until he disengaged from the group he'd been talking to, she noticed he looked around as if searching for the person he'd arrived with. The disappointment on his face meant she could go ahead with her devious plan to meet him without fear of interruption, though she'd have to be quick because other man snatchers were on the lookout as well.

She strode through the crowd until she was close enough to bump him, 'accidentally' spilling her drink all over the front of her expensive party dress. If he was an asshole, he'd blame her for the accident; if he was a gentleman, he would take the blame. A number of partygoers had witnessed the calamity but no one rushed to her aid; they merely hid behind their smirks.

He turned, a nasty look on his face, prepared to tear strips off her but once he'd run his eyes over her body and realized Mel was standing there dripping, he was nothing but concern for her welfare.

"I'm so sorry. Did I do that?" He dragged a clean handkerchief from his pocket – Mel was so glad to see he wasn't a tissues man – and began to dab at her evening dress.

People began to titter and she was soon in danger of exploding into a spontaneous orgasm. She suggested they move out of the crowded ball room away from the glares of the other women.

"I'll be only too glad," he said. "Boring bunch of farts."

They found a small private space and he dabbed at her dress with a little more purpose than before, beginning at her breasts where, as she was wearing no bra, her hard as diamonds nipples pointed the fine fabric. He moved down her torso until his hand was above her mound. Mel had sacrificed panties in order to favor the hang of the dress.

The stranger placed his nose close to her and sniffed. "My, you are wet down here." He rubbed her crotch with especial care. Mel made a sound somewhere between a peep and a moan.

"I think you need to get out of that wet dress in order that we can sponge down the accident in the front and allow it time to dry before you put it back on. Are you reliant on anyone here?" he asked.

"No one," she lied, hoping that Alex would take all the time in the world.

"I know where we can go so we won't be disturbed," he said. "I saw it earlier. Come with me"

He took her hand and after looking to ensure they wouldn't be seen, he hurried her under the velvet rope guarding the stairs. They were on the landing before anyone could see them. He tried one of the doors that looked as if it could be a bathroom off the upstairs corridor, but it was locked. Not so the door next to it. It opened to his touch. Ensuring it was empty by the light of the moon which cast a ghostly glow through the picture windows, he dragged her inside, then closed and locked the door.

Lanyon had discovered that the rumor about Alex was at least partly true. He was an expert cocksucker. After he had guaranteed there would be no repercussions to do with his employment prospects whether he did or did not suck Lanyon's rather succulent prick, Alex had dropped to his knees to lick his boss's balls. Lanyon loved it when his sex partner chewed his nuts and laved them with saliva. It was amazing how many women thought the mere idea of it was disgusting. Lanyon knew if they wouldn't do that they weren't going to swallow his junk. Those women he fucked quickly and gave cab fare home. Those that did lick, suck and swallow, he cultivated until he could have his pick of a whole ranch of beauties, mostly female but also including a handful of men.

He found the men less demanding and more amenable to the kinkier aspects of his requirements. None of it was heavy BDSM or anything at all like that but he did like to shoot a load on his partner's face or tits, plus he liked to watch them swallow his spunk after swirling it around in their mouth. He also liked to watch before joining in, and he liked multiple partners. He had little enough scope to indulge what with being a partner in the firm and what little time remained taken up with a wife and three children. He'd had the cut after the third although his wife was broody for more.

In Alex, Lanyon knew he'd found someone who wasn't afraid to get stuck into the down and dirty. He had Lanyon's balls slick with spit. Lanyon had even lowered his trousers to give Alex better access. His employee jumped at the opportunity to show his prowess by taking all of Lanyon's not unsubstantial cock into his mouth and way down into his throat without gagging.

Lanyon panted. "Oh, fuck."

He gripped the back of Alex's head and began a steady rhythm. He wasn't one of those men who loved to choke women until snot and phlegm covered their faces. He just liked a good deep throat that could take every inch of his horny cock. His weakness was that he could never remain passive while his partner worked on his prick. He knew that was the best way to go about a brilliant blow job but for him it was simply impossible. He liked to show his skill in his pumping action. He'd reached a sort of amenable mid-range between the two opposites and now Alex was the recipient.

Knowing his face was going to cop a battering, Alex relaxed ready to take the company sausage as far down his throat as he could. On a business level, Alex hated the man who was currently feeding his sexual thirst. On a personal level he'd gladly become Lanyon's sex slave. Lanyon's grip tightened and Alex was acutely aware that he needed to pace his breaths between thrusts otherwise he'd choke. Lanyon had a nice line in whispered dirty talk that was churning up feelings of lust in Alex's balls, his new boyfriend all but forgotten.

Alex had just unzipped and drawn out his own frustrated cock, taking another of Lanyon's deep thrusts as far down his throat as humanly possible, when there were voices in the hallway outside. Shortly afterwards, someone tried the door to the bathroom. Lanyon stopped thrusting and the two men froze in position. They were safe as the door was locked. They did, however, soon hear the intruders in the bedroom next door.

There was muffled chatter from the newcomers, then the sound of laughter, although Lanyon could not make out what was being said. Everything went quiet. He hadn't heard the intruders leave the room so he assumed they were still there. Lanyon was too horny to stop his activity totally, pushing his cock in and out of Alex's mouth gently, hoping the interlopers would leave soon. It didn't bear contemplating his future with the company if he were caught in the bathroom with his dick buried in a male employee's gullet. Sure, he'd plead drunkenness and gladly sacrifice Alex as a predatory queer who'd seduced him when his critical faculties were at their lowest. He was important enough to the company he knew they'd accept that explanation while not believing it for a moment.

The tension while they waited in the bathroom was becoming unbearable. Lanyon wanted to finish up and get out of there, but the visitors seemed in no hurry to vacate the bedroom. It was a waiting game. Just how badly did Lanyon want to blow his load?

Then the dynamic changed. A series of loud groans emanated from the bedroom. A woman's moans. That had Lanyon edging. He loved the sound of other people having sex. What he loved even more was watching them, particularly if they didn't know their most intimate moment was being observed. The ultimate was that Lanyon could join the people he was watching. The kinkier the action the better.

The bathroom was illuminated by the same moon pouring through the window. It would be a dead giveaway if he opened the bathroom door now. He was curious to see which of his employees had violated the no trespass velvet rope and had the gumption to make out in an upstairs bedroom. He leaned over Alex who remained kneeling on the floor to pull the shade on the bathroom window. It did much to darken the room, but not enough.

The sounds from the bedroom were more frantic than ever; the woman obviously nearing orgasm. If she didn't tone down the verbalizing she'd have the entire party up here as an audience. The moon obligingly passed behind a cloud and the room darkened further. Lanyon quietly opened the connecting bathroom door and slipped into the bedroom, dragging Alex with him. He quickly and quietly closed the door behind them.

The couple in the bed were unaware they were being observed. Lanyon didn't care if anyone knew he'd allowed Alex to chow down on his meat. It was odds-on the couple in the bed were not husband and wife or boyfriend/girlfriend, otherwise they would have taken their fucking home. No, this was as illicit as anything he and Alex had been doing.

He was annoyed he couldn't make out who the two figures were. The screaming woman looked vaguely familiar in the dark but the man had his head buried between her legs. She panted with the exertion of her orgasm but managed to rasp out, "That was great, but I need you to fuck me now."

The man remained mute but followed instructions and kneeled on the bed, his sweat stained ass positioned so that his cock was about to enter her quim. There was a second's pause before his body jerked forward and he obviously entered her cunt.

"Holy mother of God, that's good," she whispered. "Fuck the shit out of me. I need it good and hard."

The man began to pound away, the bed squeaking with his effort, the woman moaning her pleasure. Lanyon was frustrated. It was much too dark to see the action in detail. He weighed up the consequences and for a good view of the action, perhaps an invitation to join in, he'd take a chance. Feeling his way along the wall, he found the light switch and flicked it.

Three people gasped, one moaned from the sight of a large prick buried up to its balls in the wettest cunt he'd seen in ages.

It was Alex's reaction that was the most surprising.

He screamed at the coupling pair. "You treacherous bastard!"

Lanyon thought that was a bit rich. Just because it was Alex's girlfriend with her legs wide apart taking in a strange gentleman's rather impressive cock was no reason to lose it, but the man concerned turned in shock. "Alex?"

Alex had never been so humiliated in his life. His best female friend was on the bed with his boyfriend's cock wedged tight in her cunt. The bottom had fallen out of his world even after it was pointed out to him that he was standing with his cock at half-mast poking from his unzipped trousers and that he'd obviously been doing something similar with Lanyon in the bathroom before he'd been disturbed.

At least Mel had the good manners to appear embarrassed that she had been caught fucking Alex's new boyfriend although the appellation 'new' looked as if it was now replaced with 'former.' She also had the excuse she had no idea what Alex's boyfriend, either new or former, looked like and as she and the man doing a bloody good job of getting her off had not exchanged names at any time no alarm bells had rung for either.

"What are you doing here anyway?" Alex demanded.

"After you left, I decided I'd been a bit harsh and I came to apologize," Dario admitted.

"For God's sake, take your cock out of Mel's cunt while you're talking to me," Alex shouted.

The three of them spoke at once.

"No way," Mel said, gripping Dario's butt cheeks to keep him wedged inside her. She was impressed that his cock had remained rock hard during the confrontation.

"I rather like the look of where it is," Lanyon said, caring not a jot for hurt feelings. "Leave it in."

"Why should I?" Dario asked. "I bet Lanyon had his cock rammed right down your throat while you listened to us."

Alex couldn't believe he was in this nightmare. "Yeah, but he's a man. In case you haven't noticed, your cock is inside a cunt. In both senses of the word."

"So?" Dario asked quite reasonably.

Alex was almost pulling his hair out. "You're fucking a woman. I thought you were gay."

"A bit of variety never hurt anyone," Dario said, turning his head away from the hysterical Alex to get back to what he'd been doing before he was interrupted.

"Mind if I watch?" Lanyon asked.

"Be my guest," Dario said. "Join in if the lady is agreeable."

"Hell, yeah," Mel smiled. "The more the merrier."

Alex groaned.

"You can join in as well, if you want," Dario suggested.

Alex made that vomit motion with his finger and his open mouth, but he didn't storm out of the room as his brain told him to do. His cock held him back.

Dario shrugged. "Watching is fine, too."

"Enough talking," Miss Bossy Boots interrupted, "More fucking."

Alex dragged an arm chair to the darkened side of the room after he switched off the glare of the overhead light and substituted the more atmospheric and friendly illumination of two bedside lamps. He sat and watched; his gut wrenched out every time Dario sank his cock into Mel's dripping pussy. He'd never seen straight sex up so close and personal in real life before with all its accompanying smells and feelings. He'd only ever interacted with impersonal non-gay porn on his computer prior to this, and that was usually for the sight of straight cock.

He was puzzled by his reaction to what he was watching to the extent he had to remove his clothes because his cock was so insistent it wanted to breathe. He stroked himself casually as he watched. He didn't understand the correlation, if any, of the gut wrenching feeling in his stomach as his boyfriend betrayed him with his best female friend, with the sheer excitement bubbling up in his balls. He ached with confusion.

None of them was taking the slightest notice of him. Lanyon had been quick to slide his cock into Mel's more than willing throat and Alex knew she was almost as expert at deep throating as he was. No one missed him.

"I can't hold off much longer," Dario wheezed. "Where do you want my spunk?"

"Shoot it inside me," Mel begged. "I want to feel my cunt all wet and sloppy with your juice."

"Take it, baby," Dario cried as he rammed her harder in single strokes rather than one smooth motion, rocketing his sperm way up inside her.

Lanyon watched. "Fuck, that's hot."

Dario remained still for a few moments and then slowly pulled his cock free. His spunk dribbled from Mel's gaping pussy. Dario moved from between her legs, kneeling near her mouth. "Suck it clean."

Lanyon had already replaced Dario; his cock pounding into Mel's used pussy. Alex didn't care about that; he was moaning inwardly that he wanted more than anything to suck Dario's cock clean. He was much too proud to ask.

When Dario felt his cock was clean enough he climbed off the bed and walked over to Alex. Instead of the amiable greeting he was expecting, Dario grabbed him by the hair and dragged him toward the bed. Alex struggled. He wasn't bisexual; he didn't want to join in.

"Your cock says otherwise," he said coldly. "You don't want to be out and proud at work. Maybe, just maybe, you can pretend you're bisexual. Let's see, eh?"

Who was this man? Alex had been led to believe Dario was a gentle, kind lover, but here he was an aggressive, demanding top man. The problem was Alex liked it even more than the 'old' Dario.

"Lick his ass," Dario demanded, pushing Alex's face into Lanyon's butt. Lanyon reached back with one hand to pull his cheeks apart to show he was in favor of Dario's command. Alex lost himself in the smell and flavor of the moist ass as Lanyon slowed down to accommodate Alex's tongue.

"Eat me, boy," Lanyon said. "Eat my ass good."

Alex felt fingers at his asshole; he knew that touch. Dario probed him roughly. He felt a cold liquid trickle down his back and into his crevice, the perfume assaulting his senses. Dario must have found some sort of skin lotion in the bedroom and was using it as lube. Alex clenched his sphincter around the three fingers lodged in his asshole to show he was ready for cock. Could Dario oblige after he'd given Mel such a pummeling?

It seems he could because Alex felt the head of a cock penetrate his entrance. He had the breath knocked out of him as the entire length of prick rammed inside. The burn burst in his brain but he didn't care. He only knew he was in hog heaven: his ass being buggered by the man he loved and his face in the succulent asshole of his boss. Who could ask for more? Maybe, if he could just make Mel disappear.

Mel came again, shouting a string of expletives. Alex had lost count of her orgasms. That was either number three or number four. He didn't really care as long as she went home now. When Lanyon withdrew his cock, smearing it across Alex's face, Alex had a close-up view of the pink, puffy cunt that was leaking the mingled juices. It held a strange fascination for him.

"Push his face in her cunt," Dario barked. "Make the bitch eat it clean."

Why was Dario doing this to him?

Lanyon smiled, clearly liking the idea. "Fuck, that will be so hot."

Lanyon showed no concern for Alex and yanked his hair until Alex's face was centimeters from the wet pussy. Dario shoved his face the rest of the way until Alex's mouth was ground against the oozing flaps.

"Eat it out, bitch," Dario said slapping Alex's ass hard.

"Oh, yeah. Look at that faggot suck our spunk out of her dripping pussy," Lanyon panted.

Mel writhed as Alex buried his tongue inside her, his best friend. The taste of warm spunk overwhelmed him and even though it was mixed with Mel's juices, he loved the taste. He didn't gag, in fact he suctioned harder, wanting to get every bit of man spooge down his throat.

He lapped at her cunt, running his tongue up to her clit before starting all over again.

"Eat me, Alex. Eat my cunt," Mel exclaimed, wrapping her legs tighter around his head.

"You're my fuckin' bitch, boy," Dario swore. "You'll do what I say from now on and like it, whore. Understand?"

Alex wasn't sure whether he would like it, but for the moment he complied by nodding his head as best he could. Mel ground her cunt harder and harder against Alex's face until it was smeared with slime. She bucked wildly and Alex felt his tongue and open mouth flood with an unfamiliar juice. He lapped it up, not wanting to waste a drop. He'd examine his motives later. For now, he was so turned on he would have fucked a goanna.

Mel lay back panting.

"I want to fuck your ass," Lanyon said.

Mel put up no resistance as Lanyon lay on the bed milking his cock as he covered it with the perfumed lotion. "Here, sit on me, face the other way."

Dario watched Mel, obviously lacking the energy to put up any sort of a struggle, as Lanyon lubricated her ass before she squatted over his cock. He knew she'd be sore from such a big cock in her ass because she didn't have the expertise that he did – always going back for more. She lowered herself onto Lanyon's cock, pausing briefly until the look of pain left her face. Soon, Lanyon was balls deep inside her.

Lanyon took over. "Now, make Alex fuck her cunt."

Alex balked at that idea. Sucking her pussy was one thing, burying his cock in his best friend's cunt was quite another. Despite his objections, Alex was manhandled along the bed until he was within striking distance of the target. He willed his cock to deflate but his sexual emotions were so heightened his cock simply refused to obey. Lanyon reached around until he felt Alex's cock and then guided it into Mel's cunt. Alex felt the pussy flaps envelope his dripping prick and then he was inside her.

"Ooh. Fuck," Mel sighed as she looked Alex in the eye. "I've fantasized about your cock in my cunt for years. I can't believe it's happened. It feels so fuckin' good."

Alex had to agree, it did. Dario had begun fucking Alex's ass again which, in turn, pushed him deeper into the wet pussy. It may not be an appetite he'd indulge frequently, after all he was mainly a bottom, but his first pussy fuck was very pleasurable indeed. He suspected that might have something to do with Dario and Lanyon being in attendance. He was enjoying himself so much he didn't notice he was fucking of his own volition.

The three men worked in unison hoping to blow their loads within seconds of one another, and Alex didn't mind at all if he managed to make Mel orgasm. He was varying his thrusts, even thumbing her clit when he could get his hand in position. He must have been doing something right because she was bucking against him and grinding into Lanyon.

"Christ, Alex, what a waste of good cock. You should be straight. Fuck me."

He could feel the tension building up inside her and kept pumping his cock into her squelching hole while Dario was close to planting his seed inside his ass. Alex could feel Lanyon's prick rubbing against his own through the thin membrane inside Mel.

Lanyon blew his load first screaming his orgasm, which set off Mel, her cunt lips clenching against Alex's cock so that he could not hold off any longer and shot his hereto virginal load inside his first pussy. Dario followed in quick succession until the room stank of spunk and sweat. There was no way to disguise what had gone on in the room.

The quartet disentangled themselves slowly, bones creaking, muscles aching. There was a certain amount of embarrassment as Dario and Alex dressed. Mel moved to get off the bed but Lanyon pulled her back down. "Where do you think you're going?"

"Back to the party," she said.

"It'll be winding up by now," he said.

"Won't your wife come looking for you?"

"She's taken the kids to their granny's for school holidays. She won't be back for a week."

Mel flopped back in the bed, a smile as broad as the universe on her face.

"You guys are welcome to stay if you want," Lanyon said.

"Maybe some other time," Dario replied. "Right now, Alex and I have some talking to do. If things turn out the way I hope, we'll probably see you at more company parties and barbecues in the future."

Amen to that, Alex thought.

Christmas Carol

Scrooge was right about Christmas. Carol would have muttered 'Bah! Humbug!' if she'd been of a Victorian mind. She didn't need any convincing that sitting at home alone, using her ivory-hued vibrator while watching her rented male-on-male-action DVDs, was preferable to the alternative: Christmas Day with the family. Now she only had to endure her mother's whining recriminations by phone rather than in person. A successful and self-sufficient woman, unlike her obnoxious and dysfunctional siblings, she had the luxury of living an entire continent away, out of reach of family meddling.

Carol had persuaded the family that she was such a pivotal part of the corporate structure, so necessary to the day-to-day running of the giant financial conglomerate for which she worked, she had to be on stand-by over the holiday period in case of a catastrophic meltdown. She may have exaggerated a little. In reality, she was the PA to the head of the Personnel Department. Hardly likely the company was going to recruit this time of the year, but it had suited her purpose to inflate her importance not least so she could remain in her apartment for the entire duration of the season of good cheer.

Her life was just as she wanted it. Well, maybe not quite. She would not have minded if the guy with all the muscles and tattoos who lived in the apartment block across the courtyard from hers had more transparent window shades. She did like to watch a man with muscle in all the right places working out, especially when he was working that big muscle between his legs as he was now. Moisture flooded her thong as she watched the silhouette of him pumping his shaft on the blinds. She got a real kick out of being a voyeur almost as much as she did when she had a long hard cock driving into her cunt like a jack hammer.

She also wouldn't have minded if there had been just a few less gay men living in the area. Not that she was homophobic, she appreciated the eye candy even if it was a flavor she was never likely to sample, but a couple of straight men thrown into the mix just to even up the odds wouldn't hurt now, would it?

Carol was popular with the gay boys of the inner city. Most were on at least nodding terms with her while many were friends who dropped by for gossip and cocktails, or else a shoulder to cry on or an ear to boast to. Their stories sometimes inflamed her to the extent she had to excuse herself to go to the bathroom and have it out with her own aching pussy, plunging her fingers, or her faithful dildo, between her soft folds imagining it was Tom or Boze or Finn doing the honors instead of sitting in her living room going on about their new conquest.

Still, she wouldn't swap her life for anything. She was an independent woman, no matter how much that stuck in her mum's craw, or probably a dried up old spinster to her married-with-five-children evangelical sister who would ring Christmas afternoon, sauced to the gills with the supposedly non-alcoholic punch that her dad surreptitiously lubricated with enough alcohol to kill an elephant. Winnie would do as she always did, crow at her 'barren' sister, going on at such length about the joys of family and motherhood that Carol had concluded long ago she was a very lonely woman behind the façade.

No, for all its faults, Carol was living the life she wanted, even if it meant keeping the family at arm's length. At thirty-six, there was no denying she still scrubbed up pretty presentable. Certainly the men at her work must see something that appealed since they kept hitting on her, making no secret of their desire to get her into bed. Few of them, however, offered more than a hurried meal in a mid-range restaurant that catered for such clientele and then back to her apartment for a quick screw before they went home to the wife and kids.

Sure, she'd succumbed on the odd occasion; when she needed the warmth of another human body rather than the heat of her vibrator. She wasn't averse to using men at their own game. She supposed, in most eyes, that made her shallow but her mind gave a little shrug and the guilt was gone.

Besides, she didn't have time to think about these things now; she had been so preoccupied with her job and hiring the requisite number of porn videos to last over the holiday, especially those with muscle hunks, that she'd forgotten the most important thing, the turkey, her one concession to Christmas. She liked to cook it just the way her mum did, then pig out on Christmas Day but still have enough left over to last until the New Year by which time she'd be so fed up with turkey she wouldn't want to look at another one until the following Christmas. It worked out well.

Hurrying to her favorite store where she knew the produce was fresh, not thawed, she hoped they would have one left. They were pricey but worth the money. As she approached Chuck, the assistant, she spied one still in the refrigerated counter. Chuck was always pleased to see her and they exchanged a few pleasantries before he asked what he could do for her. The only other customer was a rather handsome guy talking to Sal, the second assistant.

"I'd like that one, please," they chorused in unison, indicating the plump turkey sitting in the case. It would have required the precision of an Olympic time piece to work out who had asked first. The guy, who clearly thought he had precedence, was having none of Carol's attitude of 'me first,' while the two shop assistants looked at one another as if wondering whether to call the cops. No doubt they'd seen many a violent fracas break out for much less than the last turkey during the holiday season.

Travis was all polite insistence as the two counter hands waited to see how this dilemma would resolve itself. "I do believe I was here first," he said, his voice steely with the superiority of his cause.

"But I shop here all the time," she said, with equal determination.

Travis turned to the men behind counter. They flinched at being drawn into the argument even though ultimately they would have to make the decision. "Do you have another one out the back?" He asked hopefully. "Or somewhere."

Both men shook their heads, not daring to speak. They didn't want to antagonize Carol, a long-standing customer even though they believed Travis had the moral claim to the turkey.

"Damn," Travis said.

Carol did appreciate the fact he was not throwing his weight around or assuming the moral high ground. He was attempting to find a mutually satisfactory solution.

Must be gay. She sighed at the loss of another sexy hunk to Gaydom.

"Say, how about we have it cut in half? Would that work for you?" he asked Carol. "I'd have to pad it out with more…" he was already calculating how best to make half a turkey stretch to feed the four who would be at table the next day.

"Look, it's Christmas," Carol sighed. "I don't need a turkey. I'll be home alone anyway. You take it. Wrap up a half dozen of those chicken breasts, Chuck. They'll do me."

"No, I insist you take half," Travis said, turning to address her. He'd been a little frightened of a scene earlier so had focused on the turkey rather than the woman beside him. He didn't want to be intimidated if she was a ferocious negotiator. He was pleased that she seemed very calm and reasonable. He'd already had numerous run-ins during his shopping expeditions that day; another would have sent his head spinning into migraine territory.

Shit! He knew her… "Carol," he said tentatively.

She looked at him, studying his face carefully. Her first reaction was the natural one; he was gorgeous, but unavailable. Though there was something familiar about him. Her brow clouded.

"It is Carol, isn't it?"

"Yes," she admitted reluctantly in case he was a stalker or she had a doppelganger with the same name wandering the city streets.

"You probably won't remember me. My husband and I met you at Roger's party about three weeks ago. We were introduced briefly."

Now she remembered, and she opened her mouth too readily to close it. "Of course, you were with that hunk of beef…" Her hand went to her mouth to stop any more words from tumbling out and embarrassing her even further.

Travis laughed. "Right. Everyone remembers Nico."

She more than remembered. For the next few days, she made passionate love to the man in her fantasies. He filled her like no other lover before. In fantasy.

"He's your…"

He nodded. "Right. My husband."

Carol was about to mumble some sort of apology although she had no idea what she was sorry for.

"I'm Travis," he said, saving her further embarrassment.

Of course, she remembered him now. He'd allowed Roger to parade Nico around the party as if he were his own personal property. She'd watched Travis, marveling that the guy would allow such a stud out of his sight. If Nico was hers, she'd never let him go.

Chuck cleared his throat.

"Sorry, Chuck. Wrap the damn thing up and give it to Travis. I'll take the chicken."

Travis was about to object but she gave him a severe look which made him change tack. "Look, have you got time for a coffee? It's been fortuitous running into you like this. I have an offer that might solve both our problems."

Carol was perplexed. She didn't know she had a problem.

Asking Chuck to hold both orders until they got back, but paying to make sure a later customer did not purloin them; they adjourned to a café a little farther down the main street. They sat in the cozy interior. Carol ordered a skim milk latte and Travis a hot chocolate. She hated him for not counting the calories and the saturated fats.

"It really was lucky running into you like this," Travis began.

Please don't say it. Please don't say it. Please don't say it, her mind chanted.

"Why don't you come over to our place for Christmas?

Damn! He said it.

She went on automatic pilot to begin listing the myriad reasons on why that would not be possible, but Travis got in first. "Hear me out. This is so not a sympathy invitation."

"Okay, mouth shut until I hear the first sign of something I don't like," she said.

"I know you don't like Christmas, you made that obvious at Roger's party, but we're in an awful jam. Nico's parents are coming to visit him on Christmas Day; their first ever look at his new apartment and, well…"

"Let me guess, they don't know that their son is gay as Lady Ga Ga's groove."

"That about sums it up," he admitted.

"And you want me to do a *La Cage aux Folles* and pretend to be his girlfriend?"

"Right."

"That is so seventies," she said. "So not cool. Where's your self-respect?"

"I know. I keep telling him to come out to his parents but he's Italian, thinks it will kill them. I even threatened to leave him if he didn't. I got as far as the front door and he was begging me to stay, that he'd tell them. I didn't bother to mention that I was only taking the garbage out. However, I wondered what he would do if I really packed my bags."

"But he never got around to it," Carol surmised.

"Always the excuses."

"So why pick on me?"

"Because you're gorgeous," he said enthusiastically.

Travis certainly had a way with words.

"Um, thanks." She would have preferred to hear it from a straight guy who was flirting with her, not some admittedly hot gay man looking to fool his boyfriend's parents.

"Plus, we sort of know you; you're not a complete stranger. And…"

Carol finished the sentence for him. "Everyone you know is busy on Christmas except me."

"Yeah, that about sums it up."

"As appealing as that offer is–"

And it was tempting. To be the girlfriend of the hottest man in the city. Okay, there was a little hyperbole in there; she hadn't met every man yet, but Nico was certainly up there with the best. Top ten at least. Shame he'd only be her boyfriend for the day and it would only be make-believe anyway. She hummed a few bars of the fifties number *It's Only Make Believe*, much preferring the original Conway Twitty version to the many later recordings. Although she might have the opportunity to get up close and personal in a platonic way which would feed her fantasies for a few more weeks, she was frightened she might take it too seriously and jump his body.

"Yeah, it sucks. I know."

For a moment, she thought he could read her thoughts.

She said simply, "I have plans."

"Fair enough," Travis sighed, but he passed over his business card after scribbling his home number on the back. "Just in case you change your mind."

She felt obliged to reciprocate, flirting briefly with the idea of making her number illegible or else reversing two of the digits which she could later claim was an accident. That would be childish. He wasn't likely to ring but she may get an invite to a party or two out of it. It paid to have contacts in this city.

"I won't," she said.

"I'd better get back, Nico will be wondering where I am. It was great meeting you again. We should keep in touch."

She liked the non-committal way he said 'should' meaning that if their astrological signs aligned at some distant time they might meet at a party and remember one another.

"Don't forget your turkey," she reminded him as he turned to walk away.

"Shit, thanks," he grinned. "I do feel really bad about taking the last one."

"Just remember, you owe me."

They parted if not friends then at least better acquaintances.

Carol didn't mind chicken. The food was immaterial really. Turkey just made it easy because the leftovers meant she didn't have to cook for a week.

Back in her cozy ninth-floor apartment, she kicked off her shoes, poured herself a chilled Riesling, turned on the TV to watch the news, which always depressed her, but it was a habit to which she had long succumbed. She wished she could break it, tonight of all nights because the ad breaks consisted of promotions for all those Christmas movies of forced good cheer and goodwill to fellow humans.

If I see one more promo for It's a Fuckin' Wonderful Life, *I'll puke.*

It was a pretty wonderful life, she just didn't like the way everybody had to go on and on about it.

The phone rang just after the weather forecast. She'd finished two big glasses of white wine in preparation for the anticipated skirmish. Her mother was reliable as ever. She always waited to see what the temperature was going to be the next day before she rang. It was her Christmas Eve ritual and by the end of the diatribe, Carol's own temperature would have risen considerably.

She tried to keep the sigh out of her voice. "Hello, mum."

Her mother never bothered with pleasantries, believing that as she was paying for a long-distance call she should get straight to the preliminaries.

"You married yet?"

"No, mum." Carol sighed. "Had I made that leap you would have been the first person I contacted."

"You shouldn't be too picky, not at your age. Your biological clock is ticking over fast."

"Yes, mum, I know."

The conversation kept up in much the same tone for another ten minutes or so before her mother ran out of breath and vitriol, finally telling her she should stand up for herself at the company she worked for. "It's not right to keep a daughter from her family on Christmas. It's unchristian. You tell them that."

"I did mum. They said they'll look at letting me have the week off next time."

She'd said that for the past five years but her mother seemed to forget.

"You make sure they do."

When she hung up, Carol knew the words would be the same next year and the year after until she passed forty then references to her biological clock would become moot. She wondered what her mother would find to hoist her with then.

That was one unpleasant call out of the way. Carol only had to survive the minefield that was her sister, Winnie, and then the holiday period was all hers. Winnie loved to ambush Christmas Day when she had enough sauced-up courage to ring. Carol usually let her rabbit on, with the phone on speaker, while she went about her Christmas chores, like preparing her body for the joys of vibrator sex and the fantasy of men-on-men action and a little more men-on-woman action on DVD.

Speaking of which. She went into the bedroom, finding the boxes of goodies at the bottom of her closet. She'd not indulged for some time. The month or so leading up to Christmas was one of her firm's busiest times, what with bonuses and holidays and casuals, and she put in long hours. She used the holiday period to recharge her batteries.

She was tempted to scratch open the packages now but the shiver of anticipation was enough to convince her to leave them until tomorrow. Instead, she stayed so long in her luxurious bath, pampering herself with aromatherapy salts, she had to run the hot water a number of times to up the temperature when it threatened to become too tepid.

She was so mellow when she stepped out of the bath, she was sure her bones had turned to mush. It was almost more than she could manage to stagger to her bed and flop beneath the duvet, drifting off the sleep in expectation of a wonderful Christmas Day.

It started out that way when she awoke from the most refreshing sleep she'd had in an age of Sundays. The day looked forlorn outside her window but she was snug and content. Yes, content. That was a good word to describe her life. It occasionally rose to happy and even less frequently descended to stressed or miserable. She was pottering along at a steady pace, enjoying what life threw up at her.

It's amazing how quickly Fate can change a person's mind. Carol's wonderful day turned upside down, a little like she did herself when she bounded out of bed full of energy and caught her foot in the bedding, ending up ass over tit on the floor, her foot tangled above her head. Stupidly, she put her arm out to break her fall now her elbow hurt where she'd bumped it and she was sure there'd be an unsightly bruise in a couple of days.

She picked herself up carefully, checking for sprains or broken bones then examined her body in the full-length mirror looking for abrasions. Still a fine figure of a woman, as they used to say in novels. She fingered her breasts, confident she could stave off the ravages of gravity for a few years yet. Her fingers had a mind of their own, brushing lightly across her slightly curved stomach, past the little field of tufted hair that she kept well-tended, slipping finally into the folds where she truly believed the secrets of the universe lay.

Her fingers were experts, much more so than the stray cock she brought home from time to time when her fingers and the plastic vibrator lost their attraction, but somehow the men never lived up to expectation. They weren't boring exactly in their incessant need to dump a load, or their less than fulsome attention to her needs once they'd come, but they were just a little dull in comparison to what she'd always imagined sex should be.

She didn't believe she was greedy because she wanted more.

If she didn't stop now, though, she would spoil it for later. It took all her willpower to remove her fingers from her pussy, already slick with her juices, to make herself eat a light breakfast and savor that first morning coffee. She looked greedily at the packages neatly wrapped on the settee, awaiting her pleasure.

Circling as if they had a life of their own, instead of just being inanimate objects which she had selected herself, she picked up the first parcel, shivering at what it contained. There was no forcing herself to carefully unwrap the gift; she tore at the paper like a wild animal. No recycling old wrapping paper for her.

The three rented DVD cases sparkled with forbidden treasures, the men on the cover virgins to her sigh, as she ran her fingers over the plastic hoping to feel the muscles and the bulges of the men beneath. She had two men-on-men movies and one men-on-woman, hoping that would be enough to satisfy her cravings for the day. She would take it easy, spread them out, maybe fast forward to her favorite activities if anything got too boring. She had it all mapped out. Life was good.

Turning her attention to the second parcel, her heart beat faster as she tore it open to reveal her sleek new ivory-colored vibrating plastic penis. The color had nothing to do with any racist tendencies, she just didn't fancy the idea of anything pink or blue or green entering her fanny. If she wanted demon sex, she'd join a cult.

The Vibe Mark 2.7x was a thing of beauty. Sleeker, longer and thicker than she was used to. She'd decided to expand her limits this year. Her New Year's resolution would be to experiment, find the interests that would carry her through to a comfortable and satisfying middle age.

Shit! When she flicked the switch at the base of the vibrator there was no familiar buzz, the device lay lifeless in her hands. She unscrewed the mechanism to reveal the tube was empty. She swore so violently the air was in danger of turning blue. Thinking back, she had insisted the adult bookshop assistant where she'd purchased the item, test it before she bought. She was no novice, batteries were never included with things like this, so she'd paid for a set. In her mind's eye, she saw the guy testing the machine, her own satisfaction at the feel of the vibrator, then the batteries being removed so the device didn't accidentally switch on running them flat and *fuck,* the assistant putting the batteries aside because they didn't fit in the manufacturer's box…

She'd kill that guy behind the counter. He'd been so busy flirting with her; he'd left the batteries out. She'd stuff his balls into her useless plastic tube when she got her hands on him.

All was not lost, she could always use the Vibe Mark 2.7x without the five-speed vibration, after all men's cocks didn't buzz, more's the pity. She remained upbeat and positive. Christmas was a shitty time of year and she commiserated with the millions all over the world who'd already opened their gifts to major disappointment. Hers was minor in comparison.

Looking at the large ivory rocket, she knew she'd need to better lubricate it. It wasn't gigantic but she didn't want to do herself an injury, she wanted to be able to spend the day on her back doing what comes naturally.

She picked up *Men with Muscle,* which would get her primed. She knew there was something wrong as soon as she tugged the disc out of the case: it was crusted with enough dried semen and what looked like pizza cheese she'd need an industrial cleaner to get it off. She shrieked, dropping the disc on the floor, in case it was some form of alien life. Assuring herself it wasn't, she picked it up gingerly between her thumb and forefinger, slipping it back in the case. She'd kill him, the guy at the adult shop.

Think positive.

The second DVD, *Everybody Fucks Raymond,* promised much and delivered nothing. She shook with barely controlled rage as she slid the disc out of her machine within seconds, it being an evangelical tract that someone had substituted for the real movie. So, when she opened the third DVD case and found it empty, she was not surprised. Fate was getting back at her for hating Christmas.

Not thinking rationally, Carol went to her apartment window, hoping, praying, that Mr. Muscles was home in the block across the courtyard and that even a glimpse of his silhouette would be enough to help get her off. No dice. His lights were out. She attempted to push the dildo inside her frustrated pussy but it hurt too much. Not thinking rationally, she flung the sex toy across the room, flinching when she heard it splinter against the wall.

If the assistant from the sex shop had been within twenty feet of her, she would have bitten his head off. Both of them.

She screamed in frustration, wondering whether it could get any worse. It did. The phone rang.

She had no idea who would be ringing this early on Christmas Day.

"What?" she practically yelled down the connection.

"Carol?" a voice asked.

"Who's this?"

"Travis. We met last night over a turkey. Is everything all right?"

"No, it's fucking not," she growled.

"You want I should come over? You know, to chat."

She was being an asshole. Travis was a nice man. "What do you want, Travis?"

"Maybe this is not a good time."

"There ain't gonna be a better time over this whole lousy holiday, Travis, so spit it out now."

"Well, I was just wondering if you'd given any more thought to what I asked yesterday."

No, she hadn't. She'd given him her definite, final, not-gonna-change answer. How many times did she have to tell him? She regretted giving him her number now. She had nightmare visions of him ringing every couple of hours to see if she'd reconsidered. She had to put a stop to that. It would ruin her peace. He'd think she was a bitch but what the hell.

"Travis, there's only one way I'll consent to what you want."

"Name it. We'll do anything."

She giggled in her head and upped the ante. "Okay. Here's the deal. I'll come over and play the perfect girlfriend. In exchange, you let me watch you and Nico doing the dirty tonight after his parents leave."

There was a long pause on the other end of the line. "Just so there's no misunderstanding, you want to watch me and Nico fucking?"

"Uh huh."

"You don't want to join in?"

She wished she'd made that a condition, knowing that would be the killer. But it would also make her seem desperate.

"No, Just watch. Ring me when you and Nico agree, otherwise get off my phone."

God, she was a bitch. Now all she had to endure was her sister. Then she'd have the whole holiday to herself.

If she hadn't left her laptop at work to stop herself from working unpaid during the break, she could have at least downloaded some porn. She was screwed. And not in the good sense. At least on Boxing Day she could get a new toy (*batteries included) and new DVDs. She'd panicked too easily. Sure, everything would be fine; it just meant she'd need to find something to occupy her until tomorrow. One of those tasks she kept putting off, like sorting her hundreds of porn DVDs according to cock size, gender preference and foreskin over-hang. She almost fell asleep just thinking about it.

Fortunately, the phone rang again. Carol snatched the instrument, a growl of frustration ready in her voice.

"Hello."

"I spoke to Nico and he agreed. As long as there's no touching."

It took Carol's brain a few seconds to work out who the fuck was speaking and what he was talking about. "Look Travis…" She was about to tell him it was all a joke then she remembered she had nothing better to do. Plus, Travis and Nico were hot. It would be better than any porn movie she'd ever watched. She was wet just thinking about it.

"No touching. Except myself."

She heard the hesitation in his voice. "Yeah, that's fine."

"You won't chicken out?"

"I can't say I'm not nervous. I've never done it in front of a woman. Nico's an exhibitionist; I don't dare ask what sort of audiences he's done it for."

She laughed, mainly to relax him but also because she felt something positive had come out of her lousy morning.

"I'll need to bone up on Nico's favorite colors and food and all that shit."

"Why don't I come and pick you up and you can spend the morning with him while I make dinner. We'll be eating early afternoon because his parents are not night people."

They made a time and she gave him her address, mentally calculating how to dress to impress. Though who exactly, she wasn't sure. She smiled to herself when she realized she would not be home to take her sister's call. There was a major break with tradition.

Her behavior was little short of blackmail. What if this escapade got around her gay friends, like Roger? Would they think of her as a scheming bitch? A pervert? Or envy her enterprise?

Wondering if it was too late to call the whole thing off, she managed to keep down some coffee and toast although the butterflies in her stomach threatened to force it back up again. She wanted to feel liberated but instead felt like a dirty old woman. Sure, the guys were only four or five years younger however, she was the one who'd made the impossible demands. But, then again, she was going to see real gay sex in the flesh. The prospect sent anticipation racing through her body setting her core alight with an explosion of sensation.

She wondered how one dressed for such an occasion. She shrugged. Naked would be best. Totally naked or should she be discreetly naked, taking into account the guys' sensibility? Fuck it; they'd be so engrossed in each other they'd probably forget she was even in the room. She liked the idea of being totally naked.

In the end, her choice was a simple outfit that showed enough cleavage that Nico's dad would be envious of his son but not enough that his mother would think her a slut. She was dressing for them, not to impress two gay men.

Pity she couldn't take photos of the action. It was probably too late to add that to her list of demands. Better not to push it, although she wondered if she might take a few happy snaps on her cell phone without getting caught.

She supposed they must think her request was creepy. They had to be desperate to accept. What did she care? All she wanted was to make somebody else's day as miserable as her own.

Travis, when he arrived, refused to co-operate. He was as excited and eager as she was depressed and sullen. What a way to spend Christmas: pretending to be some gay boy's girlfriend to fool his parents, then playing with herself while she watched said gay boy and his partner buggering each other. Assuming they did bugger each other. She couldn't bear it if her misfortune piled even higher and the two guys just jerked each other off. She wished now she'd looked at the fine print more closely. She suddenly realized she had no idea what was expected of her that day.

"You look fabulous," Travis gushed.

How could one stay angry against that?

She thanked him so gracelessly he watched her out of the corner of his eye as he drove off in case she suddenly pulled a knife. He began questioning whether this was such a good idea after all. He avoided turning on the radio in case all that exaggerated cheer and goodwill upset her. Instead, he concentrated on a barrage of small talk to get her mind off what was troubling her, because something obviously was.

He asked several questions hoping that they wouldn't be irritating and she would be drawn in enough to answer. It wasn't a long journey from her apartment to theirs in the gentrified, bohemian quarter. Slowly, she thawed and began asking her own questions. "All will be revealed when you get to our place. Better to hear it from the horse's mouth so to speak," Travis said, relieved she was responding to his attempts to cheer her up.

"And is he hung like a horse?" she asked then blushed, realizing much too late she may have overstepped the boundaries of what was appropriate even under these strange circumstances.

Fortunately, Travis chuckled. "You'll just have to wait to find out, won't you?"

The apartment was lavish, reeked of success and good taste. Her apartment was splendid enough, but this was superb, and that was before you included the view from the eighth floor window overlooking the river. She murmured her approval as Nico came out of the kitchen drying his hands on a tea towel. He hugged her, kissing her lightly on the cheek.

"Thanks for helping us out," he smiled. He was even more handsome and built than she remembered. A woman could get used to being pressed against that chest, held by those biceps.

"My pleasure," she lied, feeling obliged to add, "I hope you didn't think I was too brazen. It was a bit of a joke really…"

"Not at all," Travis called as he went to check on the turkey, roasting in the oven. "Nico got quite excited, he loves an audience. We had some of the best sex ever last night."

Carol looked stricken. Would they be up to performing again tonight?

"Relax," Travis called. "He's insatiable. Wears me out. He'll be in top form tonight."

"You guys haven't lured me here under false pretenses, have you?"

"Hardly," Nico said. "We're card carrying members of Gays Anonymous. Much too gay for our own good."

Damn.

Over the next hour and a half, Nico and Travis drilled her on the sorts of things she would know as Nico's girlfriend. Travis was designated his flatmate. They'd moved enough of his clothes and other goodies into the spare room that it would look real enough. They'd hidden all the gay porn, anything even remotely gay. It was tedious, but necessary, although Carol could see it rankled with Travis. He was out to his folk and couldn't see why Nico couldn't be the same to his.

The excuse she heard uttered more than once was, "I'm Italian."

He wasn't wrong. Nico's parents, Aldo and Costanza, were old-world Italians, straight out of Hollywood typecasting, and she began to understand his reluctance to come clean. She joined in with the festivities pretending to enjoy it all when she got this funny feeling that she might actually be really enjoying herself, not play acting, although she did have to pretend the superb meal was all her doing. Travis helped her carry it off, of course, as he was the real chef. She hated that he didn't get the credit, because she couldn't cook like this to save her life. The turkey had ended up in a much better home than if she'd 'won' it.

Able to deflect any questions aimed at her, the whole enterprise chugged along flawlessly. When Nico's momma went to the bathroom, after giving the ultimate accolade, "Nico, I'm so glad you find yourself someone who cook almost as good as your momma," the whole party relaxed.

"She can't have got lost," Nico said, after she failed to return for the longest time. "The apartment's not big enough."

"Maybe something has gone wrong in the powder room. I'll go look," Carol volunteered.

She found Nico's momma not in the main bathroom but in the en suite attached to her son's bedroom. She was going through his medicine cabinet.

"You won't find any drugs if that's what you're looking for." Carol could say that with the utmost confidence because she'd searched already.

"Pah," she spat. "I know that. You think a mother can't tell. Show me your hands."

Before Carol could react, Costanza, grabbed her hands and examined them closely, turning them over like some aggressive palm reader.

"You have never cooked a day in your life," she said matter-of-factly.

Carol wasn't sure where this was going but she knew better than to lie to the old woman.

"No, I'm a terrible cook."

"It was this Travis boy who did the cooking?"

"Yes."

"I thought so," she nodded wisely. "You do not live here with my son?"

"No, I have my apartment across town. I like my independence."

"Good," she said. "Whose is the spare bedroom?"

Carol went to say that it belonged to Travis but saw the look Costanza gave her.

"It's spare. For visitors. That sort of thing."

"Or to fool elderly parents if they drop by," she chortled.

"You knew?" Carol asked.

"I guessed. The second bedroom does not have the feel of being lived in. It is not enough to move a few clothes. Anyway, they leave too much evidence in the bathroom. Any mother can read her son by visiting his private bathroom. There are two people living in this room. Two men."

Costanza sat on the large bed, patting the expensive bedspread for Carol to sit beside her. She poured out the whole story while the old woman listened patiently.

"He was scared you would be upset. Family is important to Nico."

"And this Travis boy. What did he think?"

"He wanted Nico to tell you. Nico thought you would be disappointed."

"Disappointed? Pah, I have enough grandchildren from his brothers and sisters, why do I need the aggravation of more? All I care about is that my Nico is happy. His papa feels the same."

Carol helped her up from the bed, taking her arm as they headed back to the dining table.

"Will you tell him you know?" Carol asked.

"No. Let him suffer a bit more for lying to his momma."

The remainder of the afternoon went so well, Carol was sorry when it drew to a close. The funny feeling in her stomach probably went a long way to explaining that. The enormity of what she was about to do hit home with the force of a punch to the solar plexus.

At the door, Costanza turned to the three of them and said, "We enjoyed ourselves so much, didn't we poppa?" He nodded agreement. "We'll be back next Christmas, God willing."

Travis and Nico looked horror stricken while Carol attempted to hide her amusement. Nico's parents were almost out the door when Costanza turned for a final word. "Perhaps next year Carol could join us again. But don't go to a lot of trouble like you did this year. Travis. You leave your clothes in my boy's bedroom. And you take good care of our boy."

She closed the door before anyone could reply.

Travis hooted and jumped into Nico's astonished arms.

They did the washing up in silence, each of them contemplating what was to come. How would it begin? If it was awkward, it would kill the mood but Carol had no clue how to ease them into it. Maybe she should just leave.

Nico begged off finishing the wiping up, leaving the chores to Carol and Travis while he went to the living room. She assumed he was setting up, whatever that entailed. She guessed lubrication, maybe some sex toys. Travis couldn't look at her, obviously embarrassed. She was beginning to feel bad.

Nico came back and took charge. "All right, you two. No putting it off any longer. Travis, go into our bedroom and change. First rule. No clothes in the living room."

Carol was sure she heard Travis gulp before he disappeared down the corridor, then she and Nico went into the living area which now had a much more atmospheric ambience, especially with the subdued lighting. She'd be able to see everything clearly enough without the glaring obviousness of full-on electric light.

Nico had moved an armchair slightly to give it a better view of the divan without making it obvious it was a seat for watching a performance. Nice touch.

She also noticed the lube and a number of hand towels and washers stacked discreetly, ready for use. It seemed a little clinical, albeit practical.

She envied their relationship, wondering what it must be like to be one or the other of them. Travis was obviously nervous and Nico did his best to protect him, to calm his nerves, so much so that Carol felt like total trash. She took the opportunity while Travis was absent to say to Nico, "Look, I never expected it to go this far. I'm sorry. It was meant as a joke. I can see how stressed Travis is. I should go."

"No, a promise is a promise. We Italians always stick to our word. Travis will be all right. I will make sure he does not panic. And in the end it will liberate his soul just a little."

"I don't want either of you to feel cheapened."

Nico looked surprised. "Cheapened? How could that be when we are making love for a beautiful woman to watch? To see how much Travis and me love each other. I think you should go and change in the spare room. By the time you are ready, we will be ready too."

Carol couldn't help it, her heart pounded with excitement. She was really going through with this and, failing Travis chickening out at the last moment, she was going to watch in full flesh color her wildest fantasy. She would have bedded either man gladly had they been straight but the next best thing would be to watch them fuck. She wasn't sure whether she'd be able to hold back from pleasuring herself but as Nico had instructed her to strip, he probably didn't expect her to.

Carol undressed slowly, still unsure whether to flee or not as she would soon be past the point of no return, but when she was naked and felt how wet and eager her pussy was she knew she couldn't back out. Walking slowly down the corridor toward the living room, she heard activity already under way. That there would be no standing around waiting for it to start relieved her greatly. The lack of music was startling; throwing their grunts, moans and crude demands into sharp focus.

She reached the corner and paused hoping to take in the scene before the men spotted her. Nico, naked in all his splendor was indeed an awesome sight, with Travis kneeling between his legs sucking his cock. He *was* hung like a horse, she was pleased to see, between seven and eight inches by her estimation, and thick. Not as thick as the proverbial beer can that most straight guys liked to boast of when comparing the thickness of their cocks: get real guys. If she hadn't been here just to watch, Nico's shaft would have stretched her more than the Vibe Mark 2.7x she had broken apart in her apartment.

Travis had a cock that was almost as large as his lover's, what a mouthful that would make. Carol whimpered softly. Her fingers were already in her pussy, slowly working their way in and out, the tension building. Nico glanced up. She shuddered. Her body reacting instantly to the blatant sensuality of his gaze. The way he looked her up and down showed an appreciation that most gay guys could not fake. He smiled and nodded approval of what he saw then beckoned her into the room.

Travis took cock much farther down his throat than she had ever managed, or thought possible. She marveled at his throat control as he swallowed Nico down to the base. She wondered if he gave lessons.

"That's it, babe, take it all," Nico cooed. "Open up for my cock, Trav. Show Carol how you take cock in that beautiful throat of yours."

He was obviously performing for her. Not that she minded. The view was more exciting close up, so she moved across the room to the armchair and settled herself comfortably, her legs spread wide. Although there was no audience for her, Nico seemed immensely taken with her pussy. She plunged three fingers inside, desperate for relief from the nagging pulse deep inside her core, and matched her thrusts to the rhythm of Travis bobbing up and down on the huge cock between his lips.

She barely had time to get used to the incredible first view of real man-to-man cock sucking when Nico whispered to Travis who stood, squeezing some of the lube on his fingers, using it to grease his ass. Nico watched his boyfriend with admiration. "Bend over, babe, show her what you've got that turns me on so much." Travis obeyed the command; Nico parted his cheeks to press his finger against the hole, before sliding inside.

For the first time in her life she wished she had a strap-on; she'd be up that ass quicker than Errol Flynn.

Nico began directing the action. "Squat over my cock, Trav, slide down my pole so I'm wedged tight inside you.'

Travis squatted, turning his back to Carol. She didn't take it personally, though she would have liked to watch his face while he had that monster plundering his ass. He sank down to Nico's balls without any trouble; obviously used to the feel of that rod inside him. She was envious. Travis began riding Nico's cock like a bronco rider determined not to be thrown from the horse.

"Fuck me Nicky, fuck me hard. Shove your cock inside my hot ass."

"You got it baby." He thrust up as Travis pushed down. "Fuck you're so tight, babe. Milk my cock, milk it."

They were only a few minutes into the activity before Nico looked as if he was about to burst. "Slow down, Trav, I don't want to come just yet. I got something special in mind. Turn around, babe. Let Carol see."

Travis turned then slipped Nico's cock back inside his ass. Now he was facing Carol. It was the first time he'd really looked at her since the fun and games began. She looked like she was on another planet, fingering her pussy like a woman possessed. Travis knew his plan was working, much as it saddened him.

"Look at her pussy, Trav. Doesn't it look juicy, good enough to slam your cock inside?"

Travis wanted to say truthfully that it didn't, but he wasn't about to ruin the fantasy his boyfriend had going on in his head. He concentrated on the awesome feel of Nico's cock sliding in and out of his hot boy pussy, and making his own cock leak.

Nico was holding Travis's cheeks apart so he had deeper access to his boyfriend's cunt, the man cunt he would never tire of fucking. He was watching Carol's reaction. She was so turned on he knew the time was ripe.

"Come over and lick his balls," Travis suggested.

Carol wasn't sure she heard right. She looked at Nico who nodded to her. Travis may have been startled by how quickly events were moving but he was the one encouraging it. Not believing her luck, she slid across the floor to bury her face against Nico's balls, while the hottest guy she knew pushed his prick deep into his boyfriend. The action was so close she could see Travis's ass stretch to accommodate the thick shaft, a shaft she managed to lick surreptitiously as Travis elevated his ass to the head of Nico's cock before plunging back down again.

"You okay, Trav?" Nico asked.

"Uh huh," Travis whispered.

"Why don't you hop off, babe, give Carol a turn?"

Travis flinched. She held her breath for no matter how hard she wanted that cock inside her pussy, she didn't want to break up a relationship. Nico fucked Travis a few more times, then slapped his ass, the indication it was time for a change. Travis seemed to relinquish his spot with the greatest reluctance, but did as instructed. Carol gave him a sympathetic look as she positioned herself over Nico, lowering herself slowly, feeling the head of his beautiful uncut cock push into her. It hurt more than she imagined. She'd never taken a cock so thick before and obviously wasn't prepped sufficiently. She tried a few more times and even though she knew the pain would eventually subside, she felt like she would do herself an injury. To Nico's obvious disappointment, she gave up.

"Go and sit in the armchair, Carol," Travis suggested.

She did as requested, draping her legs over the arms to open herself fully, hoping his plan would work because she wanted that cock badly. "Eat her pussy, Nico. Get her ready to take you."

Nico got down on his hands and knees lapping at her pussy lips like a cat with a bowl of milk, making her writhe with the expert way he used his tongue on her clit, making her wet enough to take ten cocks.

She watched in fascination as Travis lubed Nico's ass while he was distracted then kneeled behind him thrusting brutally into him as if he was punishing his lover for his infidelity.

Travis, despite himself, was turned on watching Nico slurping cunt and was in danger of blowing his load in record time. Trying to ignore the sight before him, he rammed Nico's ass like a piston, the pressure building in his balls, until they threatened to explode. "I can't hold it guys," he warned his playmates, spurring Nico to even more aggressive tongue action. "Yes! Oh fuck!" Carol bucked wildly, shaking from head to toe, Nico tasting her screaming orgasm as Travis squirted deep inside his quivering ass, pulling out when his last drop had been deposited.

Urgently, while Carol was still coming down from her orgasm, Nico kneeled, aimed his cock at her glistening slit, and pushed. It was not the time for niceties so he sank half the length before she pushed her hand against his chest to stop him. Taking deep breaths, she counted to ten then removed her hand so he could bury the remainder of his cock inside her, down to his balls.

"Holy mother of God," Carol yelled, feeling her pussy stretched wider than it ever had been before. Desperate as he must have been to come, Nico still took his time until Carol could accommodate him comfortably. She let him know when she was ready by pushing her pelvis forward to meet him, trying to give him more depth, more feedback that he was doing the right thing.

She didn't expect him to take much notice of her needs, after all she'd already had one orgasm to his zero, but he was driving his cock into her as if daring her not to come again. She looked over to see Travis watching closely, his gaze fixed on Nico's length plunging in and out of her. He was stroking his own depleted cock which was showing every sign of hardening again. Obviously these two could go all night.

Closing her eyes, she attempted to prolong the delicious agony but it was a losing battle. With Nico determined to make her come again, and desperate for his own release it was only a matter of minutes before she groaned and her cunt began to tighten around his shaft as she met and matched his thrusts. Nico upped the pace, his efforts signaled by breathless pants. On the verge of coming, he pulled out of Carol's wet hole to jerk his spunk all over her groin, some of it spattering against her pussy flaps. He flicked the cum off the end of his cock and rubbed the slime on his fingers into her cunt.

"Come on, Trav," Nico encouraged. "Lick it up. Let me see all my hot spunk on your tongue."

Travis hesitated. Nico pushed gently on the back of his head guiding him to the spunk puddling on Carol's groin, close to her excited pussy. Travis's tongue snaked out reluctantly as he had never had sex with a woman, not that he thought slurping up his boyfriend's spunk off her shaved pussy was sex. He sucked the puddles into his mouth, the taste of his lover's sperm galvanizing him. The spunk's familiar taste and texture calmed him. He licked again, his eyes half closed, to avoid looking at her pussy even though ropes of Nico's cum glistened in her folds. He wouldn't go there.

"Hey, baby, this will help you," Nico said, handing his boyfriend the small bottle of liquid.

They didn't use drugs often when it was just the two of them but Nico would sometimes break out the poppers to help Travis relax, get into a scene. It was never more obvious he needed it than now.

Snorting twice in each nostril, he waited for the rush to hit, tasting pussy juices when Nico kissed him tenderly. It was the first time he had tasted cunt.

Nico pulled back. "You like that, Trav? You like the taste, baby? You know I need pussy every now and then."

Travis did know. He could tell Nico was contemplating an attack of pussy lust when the straight DVDs turned up from the video store, followed by Nico coming home later and later at night. He knew Nico was his and if he needed pussy every now and then, he just wished Nico could share it with him like now. He supposed it didn't help that he was one hundred per cent gay, but he could always watch.

Travis's head spun, his heart raced, Nico was telling him to eat up all his spunk. He thought he'd got it all. He wanted to please Nico. There! There were some drops of cum nestled in her pussy lips. Nico pressed his head, closing the gap, so Travis had his mouth up close to Carol's shaved labia.

"Eat it, baby, go on, eat it. That's a good boy," Nico whispered.

He held his breath, hoping the poppers had done the trick. It was so fuckin' hot watching his gay boyfriend with his face close to being buried in wet pussy, he was already hard again. He nudged his cock into Travis's already slick hole, gently easing him closer and closer to those pearls of cock juice.

"Lick it up, baby. Lick all my hot juice. Taste it, Trav. Lick it, baby, that's it, lick it all out."

Carol lay back in disbelief that Travis was lapping her pussy. He was no expert but he was still sending shivers through her body. She held his head in place as Nico encouraged, "Suck it, baby, suck it all out. That's the taste on my cock, Trav. You like that taste on my cock? Here baby," he waved the bottle, "Take another hit, maybe that will help you."

Travis withdrew to take mammoth snorts from the little brown bottle. Hoping to please Nico, he plunged at Carol, pushing his tongue vigorously into her slit. She bucked as he entered her.

"Your ass is so hot, babe. I love having my cock inside you." Nico pounded Travis hard, pushing his face into Carol's wet hole at every thrust. Travis became more adventurous, wrapping his lips around her clit, nipping it softly with his teeth, and then running his tongue over the sensitive bud. *You can do this.* Silently Travis repeated the mantra over and over. He'd do anything for Nico. That's why he'd invited Carol over in the first place. He didn't give a fuck about Nico's parents but it was a good pretense to get a hot woman to their apartment. He knew Nico's libido would do the rest. When Carol made it a condition that she watch them have sex, it had been an easy step from there to get her involved physically. He just hadn't expected to get this involved himself.

Travis came up for air, his chin shiny with Carol's juices. "Why don't you fuck Carol again, babe. I'm a bit sore," he suggested.

She saw Nico look at him strangely. She guessed Travis had never been too sore in the past but who was she to argue. She wriggled her butt on the settee, moving her legs wider apart in the process, hoping her glistening pussy would be all the invitation Nico needed. He wiped his cock before he kneeled between her thighs, and drilled his hard length into her. She took it easier this time.

Travis called his encouragement, both as an act of bravado and to prove to his lover that he was okay with what he was doing. "Fuck her cunt, Nico. Pound her like you fuck me, babe."

Their roles reversed now: Carol the exhibitionist and Travis the voyeur.

"You look so good back here, Nicky, buried to your balls in her pussy," Travis said.

"You know I gotta have cunt, Trav. Need cunt, love cunt lips wrapped round my prick."

"Go for it, Nicky. You know I'd never stop you. I love seeing your cock buried in cunt, watching you fuck pussy."

"I wanna suck your cock, Trav."

Travis moved quickly around the chair until his cock was level with Nico's face. Bending his legs a little, he jammed his rock hard weapon in his lover's mouth. Carol wasn't sure but she thought she heard Travis whisper,

"You owe me big time, Nicky," before the flush of an approaching orgasm swept through her body.

Nico might be mostly gay, but he knew all the ways to bring a woman off with his cock. She looked up at Travis towering over her, wishing he'd feed her his cock, but she was grateful she got anything at all from him and that he'd deigned to share his magnificent boyfriend, even if it wasn't for totally altruistic motives.

She writhed under the onslaught of Nico's cock until she just couldn't hold off any longer. Her body juddered alarmingly, her muscles clenching around the hard yet silky mass that filled her so completely. "Yes! Oh my God!" Carol shouted her relief as she came for the third time that night. Nico kept pumping her cunt until he too lost the battle and squirted deep inside her already sloppy hole. He fell on top of her, sucking her tits like a baby.

Travis had long since lost the use of Nicky's mouth and was desperate to shoot a second time. He stood over them, jerking his prick, spattering his seed over their faces as they lay exhausted beneath him.

They were all going to need a shower.

There was only slight embarrassment when they eased themselves apart, mainly caused by the unexpected nature of what had occurred. None of them had regrets, least of all Carol who had been invited into Nico and Travis's relationship for the night. She'd learned a lot about herself and her desires from the experience. Her life would never be the same.

"I'll drive her home," Nico volunteered after they'd cleaned up and had a post-prandial coffee. Carol saw the look of distress on Travis's face. He obviously believed Nico would take advantage and attempt to make another date to hook up without him. She didn't want that. Sure, she'd had fun but she didn't want to interfere on a regular basis. "Where do you live?"

"She lives in the same complex as Dallas, on the other side of the courtyard," Travis said.

"Who's Dallas?" she asked in an effort to avoid a confrontation between the two men.

"He's a gym bunny we see from time to time. Even bigger muscles than Nico's," Travis said.

"No, they're not," Nico sulked, showing off his bicep so that Carol drooled, almost tempted to take him up on his offer of a lift so she could get in a little Christmas car sex. Better not.

She wondered whether they were talking about her Mr. Muscles so she described her man to them. Her heart sank when they agreed that was Dallas.

"Shit." That was depressing news.

"What's the matter?" Travis asked.

"I've been fantasizing about him for months. Now I find out he's gay."

Nico laughed. "He's about as many parts gay as I am straight. Just gets the urge for cock occasionally and we're more than happy to oblige."

"How big…?" Carol felt tawdry asking such a question but she couldn't help herself.

Travis nodded in Nico's direction. "About the same as…"

Carol's mouth watered and her body heated with desire at the thought of making out with him.

"I just wish he'd leave his blinds up when he exercises so I can get better eye candy while I–"

"Too much information," Travis said, placing his hands over his ears.

"About that lift?" Nico said hopefully.

"Thanks, but I've got friends in the neighborhood and I told them I might drop in Christmas night."

She could see Travis knew that was a lie, smiling his appreciation for her consideration. It also told her in no uncertain terms that while he knew he'd made the right decision for Nico he didn't want it to become a habit. She was fine with that. She left, promising to keep in touch. That may have been a lie, although she was likely to run into them at various functions around town. As she flagged down a lone taxi prowling the late Christmas streets, she was amazed at how her initially disastrous day had turned out. She'd send a prayer of thanks to the Fates once she figured out which one was responsible.

Tired, eager to spend the next day or so recovering from one of the most intense sexual episodes of her life, she realized neither of them had kissed her. Perhaps an act too far. It had been sex, not love. Some people didn't get the difference. Still, she had enough visualization material to last her for a very long time indeed.

As she entered her apartment, weary and hungry, thankful Travis had given her a container of leftovers that would last a day or two, she noticed the light was on in Mr. Muscle's…Dallas's apartment. She went to her window, staring across the expanse that divided them, seeing his body silhouetted against the light. Suddenly, the blind raised and Dallas was staring straight at her, a phone cradled against his ear.

She thought of quickly hiding but that would be more embarrassing than being caught staring. He continued to look straight at her as he chatted on the phone. She wondered whether it was Travis he was talking to and that's why he'd pulled up the blind. She had her answer when his hand went to his crotch, squeezing it suggestively. Then he waved.

Lydian

COMING SOON

GAY DICK FOR THE STRAIGHT CHICK 6

She was hell bent for his leather.

Eve thinks she makes a pretty convincing male when she's disguised in leathers. She has a crush on Ricky, a gay guy she works with and who she knows visits The Hell Hole, a gay fetish bar, on weekends. What better way to get him up close and naked than to make a date as a biker dom. Now all she has to do is gatecrash the bar and hope he doesn't recognize her.

ABOUT THE AUTHOR

Jazmin loves sex. It's a serotonin booster, it's cheaper than a loaf of bread, and nowhere near as fattening unless you're doing it with chocolate sauce or whipped cream. The only thing better than the real thing is writing about it.

She loves sex in all its myriad forms. Sometimes she even mixes a little romance with the sex although she thinks vanilla is only for ice cream.

jazminstarrwriter.wordpress.com

OTHER TITLES BY JAZMIN STARR

Bobby's Girl

Cops & Throbbers

Great Balls of Fire

Please visit Jazmin's page at lydianpress.com

Lydian Press is dedicated to bringing you the finest GLBTQ erotic literature on the web.

Visit us on the web at:

http://lydianpress.com